Running Through the Roses

A Novel

Ken Kron

PublishAmerica

Baltimore

ISBN: 1-59286-991-2
PUBLISHED BY PUBLISHAMERICA, LLLP
www.publishamerica.com
Baltimore

Printed in the United States of America

Dedication

To my wife, Kathy, for her love
and encouragement,
and to Keith C. Kron, my twin,
to George Ki Kron, my older brother,
and in loving memory of Helen Nelson Kron,
our mom who shared much of the trauma and joy
written about in this fictionalized account
set in central Connecticut in 1948.

Acknowledgments

A special thanks
To Kathy, my wife, who read, re-read, and edited this manuscript,
To Hope Johnson who was my helpful, unofficial editor,
To Karen Hesse whose novel *Out of the Dust* inspired this story,
To my friends at the Carnegie Center in Lexington,
Neil Chethik, and Jan Isenhour,
To my daughter Karen and her husband, John Hamilton,
To my son Keith N.,
To my twin brother, Keith C., and my brother, George,
and to my close friends Harry and Roberta Owen,
Earl Pfanstiel, Carlock and Juanita Stooksbury,
Beverly Leitner, and Mary Margaret Ridenour—all who encouraged me.

Forward

Running Through the Roses is my fictionalized account of what it was like to live with an alcoholic father in central Connecticut in 1948, the year he died. Although the work is fiction, I believe the tone of the novel captures the pain, trauma, joy, and zest for life we all shared as my father, and we, encountered his demons. Four Roses was my father's whiskey of choice, and thus inspired the title of the novel. Incidentally, when my older brother, George, read the manuscript copy of *Running Through The Roses*, he said, "That's not the way I remember it," and I answered, "No, it couldn't be. You'll have to tell you own story…."

Christmas   ...1947

Dad didn't make it downstairs
for Grandma Swanson's
traditional Swedish Christmas Eve feast.

Grandpa Swanson was there
in his wheelchair.

Mitch, Aunt Edith, and Uncle Ed
walked over from across High Hill Road.

Mom, Kyle, Karl, and I were there.

The house smelled of corve, lutfish, fruitsupa, headcheese,
sill and potatoes, ("silla patatees," Grandma says,)
anchovies and sardines.

Grandpa called, "Merry Christmas!" from his wheelchair.

Dad kept us awake the eve of Christmas Eve.
He cried out,
"Get me another drink, Ellen.
I said, 'Get me a god damn drink!'"

I don't know how we would survive
if he didn't finally fall asleep at three or four!

Our old farmhouse on High Hill Road
in rural Ferndale near the water tower
in central Connecticut
belongs to Grandpa and Grandma Swanson,
but Mom pays rent, and we live upstairs.

After dinner, before I went upstairs that Christmas Eve,
I, old Kurt, sat peacefully, filled with nostalgia
in front of the tree in the living room
mesmerized by the green, red, and blue lights
and listened to carols on our old Victrola,
rubbed my lucky horse-chestnut
and prayed
a childish prayer
that Dad would forsake the bottle.

I guess my prayer for a B-B gun
was childish, too.

Before we went to bed
Kyle, Karl, and I plotted.

We'd sneak downstairs at five
to see what gifts had been left.

Our internal alarm clocks worked
even if Dad, again, kept us awake half the night
or longer.

I guess he'll go back to the VA hospital soon
to dry out.

There were games, puzzles, clothes, apples and oranges.
And new ice skates—
Karl, my twin, and I
disappointed that we didn't get
Red Ryder B-B guns to match the one
Kyle has had for years.

(We are told, "Karl, Kurt, you are too young.")

But the skates were good, greatly appreciated,
and if we had our way,
we would have gone skating
before the sun creased the sky.

Mom came down to share our excitement.
No Dad.

We skated after breakfast.
By eleven
a miracle!
Dad felt well enough,
and we went to New Britain to Grandpa and Grandma Thomas'
and to Uncle Kurt and Aunt Liz's
to get our Christmas loot:
sports equipment,
a basketball and sneakers for Kyle,

a football and sneakers for Karl,
and a bat, baseball, and sneakers for me.

I know

the gifts will

      wear out,

            deflate,

                  break,

                        be covered with electrical tape

                                or get lost

before our seasons end.

New sneakers.
There's nothing like new sneakers
for kids who run and jump and jump and run.

All in all, a good day,
but greed, and maybe dreams,
are bad.

I had my heart set on that B-B gun.

Still, I can never understand why
we have so much

when others have so little,

except my cousin, Mitch,
who always gets giant erector sets with motors,
electric trains, and man-sized walkie-talkies.

But still, how does Mom do it?

HOW DOES MOM DO IT?

New Year's Day   ...1948

We—Karl and I—went skiing today
with Mitch, our first cousin, who lives across the street,
and Brad, a second cousin, who lives on Hartland Hill,
a mile away, past Aunt Marion's house.

Some call it "cross country skiing."
We just call it skiing.

We skied down the big hill behind our house
our knapsacks on our back,
        and snowplowed up the hills
                    and over snow-covered field stubble,
                        up and down,
                                over and around,
                                    across highways and roads,
taking off our skis to negotiate fences.
We even skied on some people's yards.

We've never been fussed at,
harmless kids having fun,
but we have been envied,

I'm sure of that.

We skied to Meadow Hills Golf Course
four miles from home,
over the line in New Britain.

We lollygagged along the way, of course,

    raced,

        played hide and seek,

            wrestled,

                had snowball fights,

                    complained and shouted,

                        and called each other names:

"Bozo," "Fenwick," "Wee Wee," Poogie," "Four Eyes!"

At Meadow Hills Golf Club,
where we all want to caddie some day,
we sped up and down the tees
and through sand traps
all…, all covered with a foot of snow,
like errant golf balls.

We got too hot
and took our gloves, scarves, hats, and knapsacks off,
and then, our coats
and hung them from birch or maple trees
which made our white, trampled playground

look like
a Valley Forge encampment.

Then we ate our lunches,
ham and cheese or boloney.

Lucky Mitch
had two roast beef sandwiches
and chocolate cookies, but,
had enough cookies to share.
Our Scout canteens are filled
with root beer, grape,
lemon lime, or orange soda.

We took our time going home,
carrying our skis over our shoulders
much of the way.

Another good day
soaked through and through
and getting cold as the sun sank,
we put on coats, hats, gloves, and scarves
as quickly as we took them off
and trudged toward home.

Sauerkraut   ...January

We went to Grandma and Grandpa Thomas' second-story apartment
on Saturday for lunch in New Britain.
Dad, usually sick,
was feeling better.

Going there was OK,
staying at Grandma and Grandpa Swanson's preferred.

Grandpa and Dad eagerly talked sports
and of the good old days
when Dad was a Triple-Threat Man at college
and Grandpa played basketball
against one of James Naismith's teams,
one of the first to play the game
Naismith invented in Springfield.

Mom said little.
Grandma Thomas, less.

We kids got bored,

explored the balcony, alleys and streets
before we headed for Walnut Ridge Park.

Grandma cooked hotdogs.
Kids love hotdogs, right?
WRONG!

Not when they included BURNT, stinky sauerkraut.
Just smelling the putrid sauerkraut made me sick.

Mom gave me THAT look.
"Eat or die!"
And I did.

I got sick all over Grandma's linoleumed floor.

Score:

Grandma Thomas   1

Mom   1

Kurt   0

But it was no game.
I was sick, sick as I ever remembered,
heaving in the car on the way home.

Dad, furious, ranted,
"Why do you always have to spoil everything, Kurt?"
And I knew he had had a secret drink or two or three.

I heaved again in Grandma Swanson's bathroom.
The next morning, Mom asked,"How you doing, Kurt?"
"A little better," I admitted.
"V-8 Juice will make you well.
Dad didn't mean the harsh words he said.
You know how he gets.
He can't help it," she added.

(As if I could forget!)

"No, please, no!"
I wanted to protest about the V-8,
but held my tongue
knowing I wanted to ask
why Dad always found fault with me,
and Karl, too, but less,
and never Kyle, his favorite son.

Mom gave me THAT look.
I drank the foul V-8,
and the cycle started again
as I heaved on Grandma's kitchen floor.

I wondered why Mom did it to me.
(I wondered why Dad did it to me, too!)

I had no answers.
Will I ever have the answers?
And if I do, will I want to hear them?

Double-Ripper   ...January

Another snow,
the roads packed hard.
Kyle, Mitch, Brad, Karl, and I
hauled the dust-covered double-ripper out of the barn
and dragged it up to the road.

The double-ripper,
a family treasure built by Uncle Walt,
Uncle Ed, or Uncle Rob—
I don't know which—
when they were young,
was a long, thin, wooden bobsled
with iron-covered runners.

It must have weighed over a hundred pounds,
probably closer to two.
We only took it out two or three times each winter
when the road was packed just right.

We sat two feet off the ground,
back-against-chest, back-against-chest

our feet pressed against its running boards.

Kyle,
two years older than we twins,
drove the double-ripper with a steering wheel
taken from some old car.

It even had a clanging bell.

Four of us bent forward
leaning into one another,
and the guy in the back,
ran and pushes for all he was worth
before he jumped on, sat, and bent forward, too.

Because of its weight and icy roads
we sped down the hill,
a run-away missile,
    clanging the bell,
            yelling,
                    and shouting
as if we were about to die
and accelerated a quarter-of-a-mile
to West Lane Cemetery!

The good was also the bad.
All that weight!
It was not easy pulling and pushing the double-ripper
back up the hill.

By the time we reached the top of High Road Hill,
we had to catch our breaths and rest

before we zipped and zoomed again.

Kyle was generous,
and we all got to steer…
once.

It wasn't his double-ripper, but he was the oldest.

As the sun did its work,
the ice on the road began to melt,
and we had to watch for bare spots
which would stop us faster than hara-kiri.

With loving care,
we dragged the double-ripper
back in Grandpa's barn
until the next time.

Town Characters   ...1948

Ferndale had its share of characters:
Pick Ax, CV, Mike Segusa,
Pop Henderson, and Lady Duck Duck.

Pick Ax was riding the bus Saturday
when Karl, Mitch, and I
went to see another Gene Autry movie.

He, Pick Ax—
not Gene Autry—
sat across from us
and often rode the bus.

We didn't know where Pick Ax went
or what he did.
I didn't even know his real name.

He was a hairy, sinister-looking,
barrel of a man,
five-feet-six,

or so,
wide as he was tall.

He frightened me.

He looked like a gangster,
enormously overweight,
and mean looking,
scowling all the time,
and in my wild imagination
I was sure he was a Mafia man.

We used the dime that Grandma had given each of us
to see two features, three cartoons,
and got a free "Spider Man" comic book.

While we were standing in line
at the Music Box theater,
a boy our age, and his little sister
came up and stood behind us.
He was wearing summer shorts,
no underwear,
and, unwittingly, I think,
exposed himself,
a large hole in his pants.

We did not hesitate
to enlighten him
about his condition!

Casually, he pulled at his pants,
only to reveal himself again,
indifferent.

I'm sure
in years to come,
he'll become
a character, too.

Town characters,
in Ferndale
we've got Mike Segusa.

We knew the ice was first safe
each winter
when Mike Segusa,
the old bachelor,
dressed in a navy pea jacket,
red scarf, and a blue wool hat,
skated figure eights
around his portable record player
to a fox trot or a waltz.

He had gotten wet
more than once!

But we reasoned with Mom and Grandma
(who didn't know about his wet feet)
"If Mike Segusa can skate,
the ice is safe enough for us."

There was Old Lady Duck Duck, too,
always dressed in black,
the old, bent woman
who lived near the dam,
on Hartland Lake
and raised scrawny ducks.

We used to race our bicycles
down the hill
lickety-split,
past her leaning, beaten shack,
and cry,

    "Quack! Quack! Quack!

        Quack! Quack! Quack!

           Quack! Quack! Quack!"

I was glad we didn't do that any more,
I never liked to do it,
but I did,
because that's what we boys did
when we were together.

And there was CV,
a gentle, middle-aged simpleton
with green, mossy teeth,
uncombed hair,
who raised his arm in church
to check his broken watch.

We were not fooled.
He was telling Dr. Daley,
our Congregational minister,
"Enough of this nonsense,
it is time to go home!"

Everybody knew CV's watch was broken,

and even if it worked,
he couldn't tell time.

I must not forget "Nardo" Germini.
Nardo's our handsome,
blue-eyed
"vacant" classmate
who, the story goes,
was dropped on his head
as a child
and has never been the same,

     jerking,

       stammering,

         and convulsing.

On our Ferndale school playground
one day,
Karl was at bat
and the bat slipped out of Karl's hand
and walloped poor Nardo in the head.

Nardo was OK.
He never even flinched,
but it couldn't have helped him any!

In third grade,
Charlene Lacowski
screamed, ran around the room,
threw fits,
and pulled Mrs. Montgomery's hair.

Mrs. Montgomery had to catch Charlene
and gently wrestle her to the ground
only to hear Charlene's mother
complain that she had abused
her poor, sweet darling daughter.

Of course, I may have been partial,
Mrs. Montgomery was the mother
of twins
and I,
her third grade favorite
who had no shame,
took advantage at every opportunity.

In fourth grade,
there was another boy—
I've forgotten his name,
we called him "Polock,"
who brought a gold clam shell to school,
a naughty NAKED man and lady
frolicked inside—
we fourth graders naive enough
to think they were dancing.

On second thought,
I guess the "dancing" woman
was no *lady*!

Yes, our town had its characters
and a lot more, too.
Like Pop Henderson,
the candy store owner,
in his black suit,
      short,
          thin,
              suspicious, and
                    stingy as a penny,
who thought all kids stole his candy,
and he had no use for their parents either
fussing at all who entered
his dark, tiny, forbidding store.

And I'll not forget Cobb Garcia's mother,
a gypsy-looking lady
with her untidy house,
knotted hair,
and practical jokes.

And I guess if I tried
and took the time,
I could make a case for Dad!

He's different, too.
But, at least,
he's hasn't gone public,
and if he did,
I'd have to crawl under a rock
and die.

Groundhog Day   ...February

The groundhog saw his shadow today.
Some called 'em groundhogs.
We called them woodchucks.

Mom hated them.
They dug up her purple violets,
multicolored pansies,
and yellow-flowered cactus plants.

Seeing his shadow meant
we would have six more weeks of winter.

I loved the spring.
I loved the winter,
and summer and fall, for that matter.

I'll be glad to compromise
and accept three more weeks

     of skating,

            tobogganing,

                  and skiing.

No School Today!   ...February

We had hours of heavy, wind-blown snow last night.
No school today!
We shoveled a path to the barn
and under the clotheslines,
work that Grandpa did before
he got diabetes
and lost his leg.

Dad was upstairs,
"sick"
of course!

Mom,
our breadwinner,
could not drive to work.

Aunt Marion walked the mile
to Grandma's house
and spotted struggling forsythia
beside the road.

Grandma, Aunt Marion, and Mom
washed and hung clothes on the line,

gossiped,
drank coffee,
and ate Swedish coffee cake.

After we rested
we— Kyle, Karl, and I—
cleared the long driveway
and uncovered the fire hydrant
out near the road.
"A must," Grandpa insisted from his wheelchair,
the drifts
two, three, and four feet high.

I didn't mind the shoveling
nor the dime
Grandma gave each of us,
but I, too,
got weary when
there was so much snow.
I would rather,
in the cold, icy air,

        be sliding,

                skiing,

                        or crawling in a wind-free tunnel

under the giant drifts.

Grandpa Swanson   ...February

Grandpa Swanson lost his leg
to diabetes a year and a half ago,
gangrene.

It began a year earlier.

He was walking out to the mail box
when, he said, "My leg went numb.
I barely made it back to the house."

After that, there were tests,
and Dr. Payne said
that Grandpa had diabetes.

Twice a day,
Grandma gave him insulin shots
with an elephant-like syringe.

As the months went by,

a blister appeared on his right foot,
grew bigger and bigger
and then covered all of it.

That fall the blister broke.

The house smelled of rotten flesh and gangrene.

Several weeks later
they put Grandpa
in New Britain General
and amputated his leg
at his knee.

Now, the house smells again.

Gangrene had started in his left leg.

How I hate that smell,
one I'll never forget.

Dr. Payne was doing all he could,
but our hopes weren't high—
Grandpa stoical about it,
but then,
what else could he have been,
Grandma sticking that syringe
in him twice each day
as if he were a dartboard?

Grandpa learned to use a wheel chair,
his stump wrapped in white flannel,

and then Uncle Fritz
helped him to walk on crutches.

Grandpa fell the first time
right near the new commode
in the bedroom
installed to make things
easier for Grandpa.

It gave us all a scare,
his falling,

but after Grandpa's first fright,
he just laughed about it.

He was average height,
but stocky,
his blue eyes flashing,
his silver hair glistening,
his white mustache
stained with snuff.

Grandpa worked at Stanley Works
for forty years,
but I thought of him as a farmer,
cutting weeds and tall grass with his long-handled
grim-reaper scythe,
hauling hay into the barn,
planting and weeding his garden,
and telling us to hoe the weeds,
pull corn borers off the corn,
and pick Japanese beetles
from the grape vines
and tomato plants.

Catching Japanese beetles
wasn't so bad,
snatching them
and flinging them
into a can
filled with kerosene.

When we had caught all we could,
we'd pour the kerosene
out on the grass,
light it,
and give those little
orange and black, shiny devils
a foretaste of hell.

I can see Grandpa
bundled in his mackinaw,
hat, gloves and rubber boots,
carrying his lantern,
going out to the barn
on those cold, windy nights
to milk Bossie
returning with his pail full,
his snuff-stained mustache covered with ice.

And Grandma
would get the milk bucket
from the pantry every evening
and skim the cream off it.

After two or three days
she'd have enough
to churn the cream

into homemade butter.

We often helped her churn,
and when it was done,
she'd lift the lump of butter
and spread it on wax paper
on the kitchen table,
sprinkle it with salt,
and knead the butter smooth.

Grandpa, of course
doesn't have a cow any more,
and Grandma
doesn't make
homemade butter.

There was a time during the war,
I don't remember why,
when Grandpa didn't have a cow,
and we'd take the white margarine
in a plastic bag
purchased from Ronchetti's Market,
and break the yellow seal inside,
and squeeze the plastic bag
until the margarine turned yellow.

Kurt, Karl, and I
often tossed the plastic bag
gently back and forth
like a fragile softball
to hasten its coloration.

Now, when Grandpa is not
using his wheelchair,

Karl and I will borrow it
and take a spin
through the house
and out on to the porch,
our hands turning the wheels,
our throats growling motors.

But as I've said,
things don't look good for Grandpa,
the house smells so,
the open sore on his left foot growing
regardless of what Dr. Payne
and Grandma try to do.

Grandpa suffering so,
and Dad upstairs shouting
for his Four Roses night after night.

I'm sure Grandpa and Grandma
can hear him.

I wonder why they don't say anything about it.

Three summers ago,
when we were at Lake Congomond,
Grandma and Grandpa surprised Mom
and bought a new, expensive mattress
and put it on Dad's bed.
That was the best summer,
the last good one since Grandpa got diabetes
and Dad began drinking more and more.

Mom, Dad,
Kyle, Kurt, and I
spent a week swimming
fishing, and boating
staying at Aunt Lucy's cottage
at Lake Congomond.

Kyle, Kurt, and I
ate hot buttered toast
with strawberry jam for breakfast,
drank coffee mixed with lots of milk and sugar,
and hoped WTIC's Bob Steele
would play,
"Why The Lion Ate Uncle Albert."

And after breakfast,
we'd row over to Babb's Amusement Park
to swim, fish
or just explore around the lake.

It was on one of those trips
I caught my first bass,
a *lunker,*
two inches long!

Another time
when Karl and I were getting ready to swim,
we stumbled across a hornet's nest.
They took unkindly
to our intrusion,
and we paid dearly for it.

Dad got angry at us
for not jumping into the water,

and we meekly argued back
that we couldn't go into the water
without Mom's permission.

For once, Dad was right.

Another time,
Karl was in the outhouse,
the door wide open,
his shorts down around his ankles,
and Mom surprised him,
and took his picture.

Karl got as mad
as those furious hornets!

Somehow that photo
has mysteriously vanished,
but we all know
that Karl is the sorcerer
who made that photo disappear
faster than
a magician's rabbit!

Even now,
as I sit on the kitchen porch
watching the lightning
as a winter thunderstorm rolls in,
I can hear Grandpa headed out my way
in his wheelchair,
looking, I bet,
for his can of snuff.

School ...February

School isn't so bad this year,
Miss Clark, a former WAC,
is our Ferndale eighth grade teacher.

We thought she'd be tough as leather,
but she's an inconsistent disciplinarian.

She taught math, reading, social studies,
geography, health, and spelling.

During recess, we guys played
softball, basketball, or football
or shot marbles—
we called them agates
and "aggies"—
on the muddy playground.

Mrs. Lutz teaches music once a week
and privately teased me
about singing off-key

so I hummed when
singing mattered.

We ate sandwiches, and drink white milk
in our classroom at eleven-thirty,
my standbys:
peanut butter, jelly, and mustard,
banana, or egg salad.

Karl was a tuna fish man.

School started at eight-fifteen and ended at three.
Karl, Mitch and I caught the school bus
on Chamberlain Highway
at the corner of West Ridge Road
near Cobb Garcia's house.

Kyle's a sophomore at Blue Hills High,
our school next year
when we'll catch the bus on Alling Street
in front of Mr. Alling's old barn.

To be honest,
I'm not a bad student,
but not the best either.

Karl, who cares less,
usually gets a grade lower
than me.
If I get a B,
he'll get a C.

If I get an A,

which I usually get in
math or history,
he'll get a B, a B-, or a C+.

Mom said I have drive,
but I think it is curiosity, too.
I like to read and write,
and my knack for memorizing
gave me an edge
in history and math,
my best subjects.

Next month
Miss Clark is taking all twenty-eight of us
on a school bus
to Yale's Peabody Museum
in New Haven to see the dinosaur bones
and an art exhibit.

She teased
and told us
she wanted to civilize us
and force some culture
down our throats.

Albert Tanner won't get to go,
and he probably needed it more than most.
"Two dollars is hard to come by,"
Albert said, and laughed nervously,
his father hurt in an industrial accident
at Paper Goods Manufacturing.

When I was six,

Uncle Ed, Mitch's Dad,
loved to try to stump me
with math problems,
much to Mitch's envy.

But turnabout's fair play,
I wanted Mitch's erector set.

And at the bus stop each morning,
the big Poppel brothers
would taunt me,
"Hey, Gargantua!"
until I flew into a rage,
and justified their jeers.

First grade was unkind to me:
whooping cough, chicken pox,
and pneumonia.

I missed so much school,
there was talk of making me
repeat first grade.

But having a twin helped.
They didn't want to separate
Karl and me,
to my good fortune.

A year earlier,
Kyle took private dance lessons
from his,
and then, our

second grade teacher,
Miss Phillips,
something I'm glad to say,
Karl and I avoided,
a sentence worse than death.

It was in second grade, too
that Whalen Sauls got sicker and sicker
month after month,
the bandage around his head
getting larger and larger
until a brain tumor got the best of him—
the same thing that had killed
Uncle Fritz's wife, Stella,
two years earlier.

I remembered them every time
we went to West Lane Cemetery.

Fifth grade was
the most memorable class of all.
There, I was Miss Winterberry's favorite, too,
but in February
she fell off a ladder,
broke her leg,
and we had a substitute teacher,
Mrs. Starnes, for the rest of the year.

Miss Winterberry was something else.

It seemed to me, hour after hour,
we'd practice our handwriting,

making

    slashes and ovals,

        oval and slashes,

            slashes and ovals
until I hated them.

(I think that's why my handwriting
is so bad today!)

Mrs. Winterberry made Albert Tanner, or Al,
sit under her desk for misbehaving,
and then sat at her desk to imprison him,
another taste of hell.

Once Mrs. Winterberry
asked the class how Al could have improved
delivering a poem we had to memorize—
"The Village Blacksmith"—
and I impishly answered,
"He could have zipped up his fly!"
and all my classmates howled.

Mrs. Winterberry laughed, too,
a big surprise.

I think I know why I was a favorite,
the teacher's pet in third and fifth grades.
I was "cute," full of playful mischief,
and a teacher pleaser.

Last year,
in Mrs. Zack's seventh grade classroom—
maybe I shouldn't admit it—
I thought I was in love
with the pretty
Maureen Andrewlevitz,
but, my heart's pitter patters
were not exchanged,
Maureen in love
with a classmate athlete.

Anyhow, school's OK,
good, in fact,
but for all that,
I'd sure like another snow day
to ski, toboggan,
and, if we are extra lucky,
to race the double-ripper
down High Hill Road.

Frozen Water Pump   …February

"Come here, Kurt,"
Kyle called.
He was standing near
the old, black, cast iron pump
beside the once-proud slate-roofed summerhouse.
and taunted, "I bet you can't kiss this pump.
You're chicken!"

Seldom to turn down a dare,
I said,
"How much?"
"Five cents"

"You're on!"

The skin of my lips
stuck to the pump,
my kisser on fire.

"You don't get the five cents,"
Kyle wickedly laughed

and mocked,
"We didn't shake hands on it."

Kyle, of course, was bigger than me,
but I attacked him anyway,
as he knew I would,
and sneered, "Here, Fenwick,
here's your nickel."

Skating at Hartland Lake   ...February

A black ice day.

The new ice
over some of last week's open waters
is thin, bending,
black and hard.
We sail over it
as if we have wings,
the silver blades of our new,
Christmas skates
dance
with slash and speed.

"Free, free," I think,
as we race on and on
up the lake
into the narrow
grassed-tufted channels
until our feet ache with cold
and we run home,
skates over our shoulders
on stumps called legs.

Dad Goes to The VA   ...February

Peace and quite.
sound sleep,
except for the nightmares.

Yesterday Mom took Dad to the VA hospital
in Newington
to dry out again.

It was time!

It used to be
that he'd go every year or six months,
then every four months, or so.
Now it's every three months,
or less.

I don't know what they do to him there,
or what he does.
I imagine they take away the booze,
have talk sessions,

and pat each other on the back
as the days go by
that Dad's more like his old self.

I'd like to know, but
I really don't want to know either.
It's Dad's problem.
Let him deal with it.

We Visit the VA　　　　　...February

I liked the peace and quiet at home
when Dad was at the VA Hospital.

But I hated the visits.
Mom took us on Sunday afternoons.
Hours of nothing to do.
To go inside,
we'd have to be sixteen.

So Kyle, Karl, and I sat and read in the '41 Chevy
or played catch on the manicured, empty lawns
with a softball, tennis ball, or football.

We had to be quiet,
no yelling and shouting.
"It's Sunday, you know!"

I don't know about Kurt and Karl,
but I dreaded the moment Mom
led Dad out
to say, "Hello."

They came,
he in bathrobe, pajamas, and slippers.
He looked a little less thin,
less white,
less wild,
his hair combed,
his face shaved.

"Hello, boys," he said,
and that was it.
He had nothing to say to us,
and we,
at least, I,
had nothing to say to him.

Mom chattered and bragged a lot.
"The boys are doing well in school."
"Kyle wrote your Aunt Lucy a letter."
"They do the chores around the house,
shovel snow, wash dishes, and make their beds."

He nodded—
The seconds dragged into minutes.

"Time to go!" I wanted to scream.

Eventually, but not soon enough,
Mom led him inside,
and we resumed our reading or our catching,
and I sighed in relief.

In fifteen, twenty, or thirty long minutes,
Mom came out, alone,
said, "Didn't Dad look good?
He loves you so!"
and we went home
to Grandma and Grandpa's house
to blessed
peace and quiet.

Father Murphy   ...February

Our visits to the VA had one saving grace.
Father Murphy, a chaplain,
patiently searched for us,
and told us a tall tale,
each Sunday a different story.

Last Sunday's was "How I Lost My Ear in WW I."

Father Murphy, being Catholic
and all,
surprised me.
He had a sense of humor,
and could laugh at himself.

We were Congregationalists,
so we didn't know any Catholic priests,
and Mom was always fussing at Catholics,
and especially Catholic priests
even if Aunt Edith and cousin Mitch went to mass each week,
Aunt Edith, I think,
to ask forgiveness

for just one son,
failing to increase the Catholic multitudes.

"Well, Kurt, Kyle, and Karl,
how ya doing today?" Father Murphy would start.

And after a little chat,
Father Murphy began:

You know I how I lost this ear?
We were on the battlefield during WW I.
The Krauts were across the trenches.
Because I was a Chaplain,
and didn't carry a rifle,
my job was to scrounge extra food...,
when, of course, we Yanks and Krauts
weren't trying to kill each other.

Well, it was our lucky day.
I came across a field filled with cabbages.

You did notice, didn't you,
that I've only got one ear, boys?

Anyhow, I gathered as many cabbage heads as I could,
and the men and me,
we had cabbage every way possible.

We made coleslaw with vinegar and sugar.
We mixed it with our meat
and had cabbage stew.
Some even found a way to make kielbasa,
a Polish sausage wrapped in cabbage!

When we finished eating,
there were still many heads of cabbage left.
I didn't want them stolen,
or eaten by rabbits,
so I stuffed them in my sleeping bag.

That was a big mistake, boys!

You did notice I only have one ear, didn't you?

Well, anyway, I guess those rabbits
didn't take too kindly
to us eatin'
and me hiding cabbage heads
they thought belonged to them.

During the night,
I don't know exactly WHEN
or HOW,
A big, angry buck rabbit,
I guess,
chewed off my ear down to my sideburn.

I tell you,
Karl, and Kurt, and Kyle,
that was some mad rabbit!

And with that, Chaplain Murphy,
out-laughed us,
enjoying his tall tale as much

or more than we did.

"Tell another," we would beg,
but Father Murphy
always shook his head,
No.

You'll have to wait until next time, boys.
You see I've got others who want to hear my story, too.
We can't be selfish, can we?
Why,
that would be rather rude!

And the good priest would laugh again,
shake our hands,
and say, *"Your Dad is doing pretty good.*
I'll pray that he will do better this time."

And then he'd turn,
walk away,
and wave to us one more time
before he limped back into the somber hospital.

Skating at the Marsh   ...February

"Let's go skating, Cobb,"
I called my classmate after school.
"I'll be right down."

West Ridge Lane was covered with snow.
"No bike today," I thought,
and walked toward Cobb Garcia's house
knowing Simpson's dogs would frighten me,
and Cobb's German shepherd, Wolfe,
would not welcome me.

I've been attacked by Wolfe,
more than once.
And Simpson's dogs chased me, too,
when we caught the school bus
on Chamberlain Highway.

And then there was Bush Wacker,
the Doberman pinscher!
I worried about him when I walk to Brad's house
up on Hartland Hill.

He attacked me twice
and got me once,
ripping a mouthful out of my leg,
a generous bite that required
eight painful stitches
and a tetanus shot
after his owner had called,
"Bush Wacker won't hurt you, Son!"

I loved dogs,
but they didn't love me.
Each thinking I was an intruder
or lunch.

Brad's dog, Button, nipped at me,
and his neighbor's dog,
another German shepherd,
sought me out
if for nothing else
but to torment me.

Those dogs!!
They were rather petulant, I thought,
and wondered
what it was about me
that made me so delectable.

Cobb greeted me,
and his little sister, too.
Ruth Anne, six.

Wolfe was on a leash,

and sniffed my leg, and
                eventually,
                        grudgingly,
accepted my presence.

Cobb and I ran down to the marsh edge,
hurriedly put on our skates
and raced up and down the channels,
some wide, some narrow,
lined with marsh grass
frozen in the ice
which made us trip
if we weren't careful.

I loved Cobb's marsh,
the perfect place for skating,
the ice the first to freeze
in the entire neighborhood.

And because the water was so still and shallow,
it was the best ice, too,
hard, smooth, and black.

Cobb and I played tag,

                darted in and out,

                        through,

                              around,

                                      up and over

tufts of grass,
Wolfe barking,
until Ruth Anne

dragged her sled onto the ice,
and I pulled the bundle of happiness
around the ice
as if her sled
were a yo-yo on a string—
Ruth Anne's laughter,
shrills and shrieks,
reward enough.

Before I thanked Cobb and left
we went into his farmhouse,
with its dark, cluttered, foul-smelling rooms,
and I wondered why
they were so untidy.

Cobb's mother was there,
she welcomed me,
but she was a strange one.
She reminded me of a gypsy,
her hair severely knotted on her head
covered with a babushka,
her shoulders wrapped in a man's suit coat.

She was pleasant enough,
and we drank hot chocolate,
but I knew
I wouldn't want to confront her
on a dark, cold night
not knowing she was Cobb's mother.

Last Halloween
at Mitch's party,
we played Pin-the-Tail-on-the-Donkey,
and were drinking cider

and eating cinnamon-covered donuts
when this strange masked man walked in,
sat in the corner on the floor,
nodded, but said not a word.

It didn't please Aunt Edith, Mitch's mom,
one bit,
a fussy, nervous woman at best!

We all wondered who the strange,
frightful visitor was,
and it wasn't until the party ended
that the stranger unmasked himself
and revealed she was Cobb's mother.

Aunt Edith fussed at her friend,
"You scared me half to death."

She, the gypsy-like woman,
thought it was the best joke ever.

I did, too,
but Aunt Edith,
I'm sure,
thought it rather rude
to scare her so.

Two years ago
at a Halloween party,
one of our classmates
peed in the cider
and got all the girls mad at us,

but that is another story.

Cobb's father,
a handyman,
went from farm to farm
and business to business
to do odd jobs.

Besides planting a big garden,
and keeping bees,
Mr. Garcia raised thousands of chickens
in house-sized coops
near the marsh.

I've heard he does quite well
when times were good
and prices were right.

Cobb's father was the man
who, each fall,
came with his tractor
which pulled his conveyor belt saw,
and cut our broken branches into logs
for Grandma's kitchen stove.

For months,
Grandpa, when he was well,
and now, Karl, Kyle, and I,
dragged wind-downed apple branches,
elm branches,
and anything else we could find
up near the chicken coop,
and then Cobb's father

built a sawdust pile,
the huge saw blade spinning
and screaming its hateful cry,

Wrannng! Wrannng! Wranng!

Wrannng! Wrannng! Wranng!

Then, we boys, Karl, Kyle, and I,
using axes and wedges,
split the wood
into stove-sized logs,
carried them to the woodshed,
and piled them until there was another cord,
enough for winter—mild or severe.

I walked home from Cobb's house,
tired and happy,
mindful of Simpson's dog,
and hoped Grandma Swanson
would have something good for supper.

Where for Art Thou, Romeo?   ...February

Romeo, six-years-old,
is a full-blooded mongrel,
the son of Uncle Fritz's
black mongrel, Theodore,
another Casanova.

Romeo disappears in the late winter
and returns a month later.

He's been gone two weeks now
but will come home, worn out,
beaten up,
pleased with himself.

Grandma has a white spitz,
Mitsi, a temperamental dog
who puts up with Romeo
who is well aware that Mitsi's nip
is worse than her bark,
and that she, Mitsi, is the queen,
tolerating but not encouraging
Romeo's playful good-naturedness.

There are cats, too: outside cats,
barn cats, and woodshed cats
that keep the rats and snakes away,
and will, occasionally,
begrudgingly,
tolerate a back scratch or a belly rub.

Comic Books and Trains   ...March

Dad's been home from the VA
ten days now.

He's thin and white
but feeling better.

Late Friday afternoon
he "borrowed" the '41 Chevy,
and wearing a jacket, a white shirt,
gray slacks, and loafers,
called,
"Boy's, let's go get some comic books!"

My "beloved" Dad wasn't fooling me,
I had heard that siren call
too many times before.

He drove to Pop Henderson's
and bought us
three comic books each,

"Archie," "Porky Pig," "Batman,"
and the like.

"You can read your comics
while I talk to my friend,
Pete Zanardi," he said and smiled
as he turned the car on Main
toward old Route 72.

I knew he means,
"We're going to the Big Dipper Bar and Grill,
and I'll hoist a Red Fox Beer,
or two, three, or four
or more."

In the dark, fly-filled grill
we read
our comic books
and played "21" with someone's
forgotten pack of cards—
the King of Spades missing.

Dad went back into the bar,
talked to Pete Zanardi,
the bartender,
and hour after hour
dragged by,
his comic book bribe "sweetened" with hamburgers and root beer.

While we ate,
Dad hoisted another "ice cold one,"
lit a cigarette,
and the flaming match head

flew across the table
and struck my left eye.

"Ohhhh! Ohhhh!" I cried,
rubbing my eye
and jumping up and down.

"Here, Son,"
Dad said,
with no apology,
"wash it out with ice water,"
and dipped a napkin into a glass.

As soon as he realized
that I'd survive, Dad plotted,
"We won't tell Mom!
You'll be OK,
a big, tough boy like you.
Our secret,
it will only make her worry."

How I hated Dad's adventures
with "my three boys!"

On the way home,
I nervously looked out the back window
and wondered if Constable Kornichuck
would see our weaving car
and arrest Dad.

The next day
he said to Mom,

"Ellen, I'll take the kids on an 'outing'
so you can have some rest."

I had another word for it,
but I would have had to use some of the words
Dad shouted at Mom almost every night.

Saturday afternoon was just as bad.
We, Kyle, Karl, Mitch, and I,
were playing baseball jackknife
under the big maple,
one we tap for syrup on our front lawn.

"Boys let's go get some ice cream,"
Dad called.
"My treat."

Mitch, of course,
who didn't know,
hopped into the Chevy
as if he hadn't eaten
in three months.

"I've got to run an errand,"
Dad slyly said,
"Here's some money
for comics and ice cream cones
with chocolate shots.
I'll be back in a minute."

Mitch, who had everything,
(that erector set,

a Lionel Train with real smoke!)
thought he had
died and gone to heaven.

We went into Pop Henderson's store
and looked for comics we hadn't read,
and got vanilla, chocolate,
pistachio, and maple walnut
ice cream cones
covered with chocolate shot,
and paid the unsmiling
Pop Henderson
and extra penny each
for his stingy, chocolate sprinkles.

Dad walked across the street,
and went into the package store,
and I saw him
slip a brown paper bag
into his jacket pocket when he came out.

"Let's go look for freight trains,"
he said heartily,
a suggestion I have heard too many times.

Dad parked the car
near the railroad underpass
and while we looked for trains,
tossed rocks into the water under the bridge,
and sat beside the creek
reading our comic books,
I saw Dad in his car
chug-a-lugging from his Four Roses pint
as if he were a kid

drinking Grandma's root beer.

I hated those trips,
but Mom insisted we go.
"It's a time to show your Dad
how much you love him," she always said,
but I worried that Mitch,
or whoever tagged along,
would learn *our* secret.

*"Sure, Mom, the more he drinks,
the more I will love him,"* I thought,
but, of course,
I couldn't tell her so.
and wondered why
she let him do it to us.

I don't think I will ever understand.

Dinosaur Bones and More   ...March

Miss Clark took our class
to Yale's Peabody Museum in New Haven.

We saw more than brontosaurus bones.
We saw those, too,
many different kinds
made to look as if
the dinosaurs were
                    eating,

                run   running,

                        fighting,

                            flying.

Colossal bones,
mammoth bones
and tiny ones
no bigger than a wishbone.

But when Karl, Mitch, and I
took a shortcut
from the museum
to the art gallery,
we passed an open classroom, and there,
in front of a room filled with eager students,
was a naked female model
posing for an art class.

We didn't tell Miss Clark
ALL
we learned and saw
when she had us write
about our trip to New Haven.

Karl   ...March

Karl, my twin,
is the best friend I have,
but when I talked about best friends,
I thought about Brad or Mitch.

The truth was
that I thought of Karl
as a twin brother
rather than the friend he was.

We didn't always have the same interests,
but we shared a lot in common:
Boy Scouts, winter sports,
baseball, basketball, football,
and hiking, camping,
and biking.

We also tried to get the best of Kyle
and shut out Dad's cries
at night.

I should tell how Karl
got spanked in first grade
for trying to see a girl's panties,
and how he got rid of the photo
Mom took of him sitting in the outhouse.

I have a million such stories.
One of my favorites was of Karl,
when he was five,
being chased around Grandma's house
by an angry Rhode Island Red.

I'll never forget that,
the big, feisty rooster
running after Karl,
my twin's tiny legs
churning faster than a paddle wheel,
he,
        running and

           shouting

              and crying,

around the house once,
around the house twice
until Grandpa Swanson
ran out with a broom
and knocked that red rooster
from here to yesterday.

That rooster didn't know
what hit him,
and two or three days later,
we ate that fat, Rhode Island Red

dressed with Grandma's special stuffing
for Sunday dinner.

There was that time
Karl went on a Scout camping trip,
and while chopping wood to build a fire,
he carved a V-shaped wedge
out of his hand
between his thumb and forefinger.

He should have gone to the doctor
for stitches,
but Karl bandaged it
before anyone could see
how badly he had hurt himself,
and today,
he has a big angry scar
to show for it.

Karl and I are competitive
in most things—
not at school—
but in about everything else.
He's a better baseball player than I,
but I'm a better
football and basketball player.

Karl's the better skier.
but I'm a better skater—
both roller-skating and ice skating—
although he would disagree.

It bothered me

that the pretty girls seemed to like Karl better,
and he has a *best girl*.

Karl and I
are almost equal in strength,
height, and weight.
We're 5' 6" and 129 and 132 pounds.
When we get mad,
and fight or wrestle
the one who gets the maddest
usually wins…although,
(and I'm not partial!),
I think I'm a little stronger.

Last year Karl and his friend, Herb,
were playing on a bulldozer and road grader
parked aside the road,
and Mr. Alling called
Constable Kornichuck
and told him that there were kids
vandalizing town equipment.

Nothing came of it,
except Karl and his friend
were embarrassed
when Constable Kornichuck
brought them to face Mom.

But Mom didn't get as angry
as I thought she would,
and I heard her and the constable
laughing about it
after she sent Karl to his room
and Herb back home.

Neither Karl nor I
had had much use
for Old Man Alling
after that.

Karl is my best friend,
and I his,
but we'd deny it,
and he'd say,
"You're nuts!"
if I said such a thing out loud.

Whiskey Cache   ...March

Karl, Brad, Mitch and I
were playing war games
behind the tombstones
in the West Lane Cemetery.
It was about 10:30 on a Saturday.

I had already cleaned the chicken coop,
and Karl had spread burnt ashes
on the icy paths
and brought in wood for Grandma's stove.

"Look," Karl shouted up to us
from the edge of the cemetery
where the fence and woods met,
"I've found some whiskey bottles."

We counted.
There were nine whiskey bottles,
most unopened hidden underneath some brush.

"Let's use them for target practice,"
Brad said,
and we lined them up
on the top of the fence
and threw stones at them,
until we had proudly
shattered each of them,
their noxious fumes,
we imagined,
gladdening those
decomposing in their cold, cold graves.

We ran up the hill,
and began to play Cops and Robbers,
until Karl yelled again,
"Someone's coming!"

We heard the clomp, clomp, clomp first,
and then saw Mr. Josephowitcz,
the immigrant, Polish farmer
who lived behind us
on Chamberlain Highway,
wearing his mucking boots,
faded, dirty, bibbed overalls,
a flannel shirt that looked even worse,
and an old ear-flapped hat.

He trudged along the trail that ran
through the woods behind the cemetery
and connected with High Hill Road.

Quickly we ducked
and hid behind the tombstones.

Mr. Josephowitcz didn't see us
and went directly to his whiskey cache.
He looked up the hill,
shook his head sadly,
turned and walked past us on the path
mumbling,

    "Sumnabitch...

        sumnabitch...

            sumnabitch."

Brad said after the old farmer disappears into the woods,
"I'm glad we broke those bottles,"

But I wondered.

He had never done us harm,
and once,
when the tire on my bike went flat
In front of his farm house,
he came out and helped me
patch the tire,
fetching the tools, a patch, and glue
from his barn.

I wondered, too,
if, like my father did to Mom,
he kept Mrs. Josephowitcz awake all night
demanding another drink.

Eye Patch   ...March

In first grade
I had to wear an eye patch
to strengthen my right eye.
I had amblyopia,
or "lazy," eye,
a condition that caused my left eye
to work overtime while
the right one lazed about.

The stigmatism in my right eye
didn't help.

I had to wear glasses
and put an opaque patch
over my left eye
to make the right eye work harder.

When I didn't wear my glasses
and the opaque patch,
I wore
a rakish, black pirate's patch.

I enjoyed the attention,
but I didn't care for the teasing,
especially by the Poppel brothers
at the bus stop.

I was
   "Gargantua,"

      "Pirate Pete,"

         "Blue Beard," and

            "One-Eyed Jack."

I'd run at them,
angry, crying,
my arms flailing,
and they'd laugh,
and intensify their sport.

THEY,
the teacher and my Mom,
talked of making me
repeat the first grade…

Dad, the Legend   ...March

I want to be fair to Dad
but it is hard.

Dad was a super athlete.
As a teen, he won the New Britain tennis title,
and he and Grandpa Thomas
captured the city's doubles title.

He was an All-City
high school athlete.
At least that's what Uncle Kurt,
his brother, told us,
describing a god-like man I didn't recognize.

It was in college
Rockwell College, in Vermont,
the All-American found his niche.
He was on the yearbook staff,
on the debate team,
a popular fraternity brother.
He even acted in a play or two.

But it was in the gym and on the playing fields
he became a legend,
captain of the football team,
co-captain of the tennis team,
the best sprint
and high jump man.

And, if that wasn't enough,
he played on the basketball team, too.

I don't know how he found the time!

After college,
he taught at an exclusive New England boys' school.

The war came,
WW I, and he joined the Navy
as an Ensign,
and it was there
he distinguished himself,
a larger-than-life war hero!

I don't know what kind of ship it was,
I guess a battleship or light cruiser.
His ship was attacked,
besieged, and bombarded.
The ammunition magazine
received a direct hit
and exploded,
engulfed in fire and black smoke.

The fire spread to most of the ship,
and shrieking men,
wrapped in flames,
were trapped below deck,
according to Uncle Kurt.

"Abandon ship," the Captain cried.
But Dad wouldn't!

"Not until we get the men out
from below,
Sir!"

"Abandon this freakin' tub,"
the Captain cried again.

Uncle Kurt, a veteran himself, said,
"Your Dad drew his pistol
out of his holster,
pointed it at the Captain,
and shouted,
"Not, until we rescue

the men,

     our burning,

          crying,

              dying men,

                    Sir!'"

Several 'swabbies' owe their lives
to that brave and reckless man,
your Dad."

There was a hearing,
after the crew was rescued,
and the smoke cleared.

"Your Dad,
my brother,
our hero,
received a Navy medal for heroism."

And I wondered, as Uncle Kurt,
my namesake,
told the story,
where and when

        that man,

           that Ensign,

                that hero,

                    OUR DAD,

had disappeared?

Another Dad   …March

I remember a different Dad.

The Dad, who,
several years earlier,
had shouted at me
on the beach at Rocky Neck,
"God damn it, Kurt!
Can't you do anything right?"
when my melted orange Popsicle
had broken and dropped orange ice
on the brown blanket we were sitting on.

Or the Dad who,
when Karl and I
were having a
corncob fight
underneath the barn,
grabbed us,
pulled down our shorts
and

whacked,
      welted, and
            wounded us,
his belt an uncoiling cobra.

To this day,
I don't understand why.

Neither do I understand why,
when Karl and I were having a rotten apple fight
underneath the apple tree
near the chicken house,
he beat us with his belt again.

There are so many things I don't understand!

Why, when I climbed the cherry tree
for the hundredth time,
the last time,
he yelled out his upstairs window
at four o'clock
one Saturday afternoon,
"Kurt, get out of that god damn cherry tree!"

I wondered if he thought if I was spying on him.

All I was doing was picking
the few dark red, sweet cherries
the raucous jays had left behind!

I wouldn't have spied on him.
I really didn't want to know

what he did up in his bedroom alone
all day.

I assumed he slept,
so he could keep us awake most of the night.

Then there was the time,
he must have been feeling better,
we twins were six, Kyle eight,
when he hit ground balls to us on the front lawn
between the cherry and the huge maple tree,
and I bobbled a grounder,
and he angrily yelled,
"Kurt, you can't do anything right.
You are the most pitiful player I have ever seen."

And the time I had that patch over my eye,
only to hear him yell,
after I brought him too-dark toast,
"God damn it, Kurt,
you're as hopeless as
an ostrich in an outhouse.
You're nothing but a handicapped fool."

When Mom and Dad got their new Chevy.
a week or two later,
I tried to roll down the back window
and it wouldn't go down.

"The window won't roll down,"
I said,
and Dad's angry words
struck me in the face,

"God damn it, Kurt,
do you have to break
everything you touch!"

Those were bitter, angry words, and hateful times.
I don't understand his hatred.
I didn't know what I had done.
Karl had made errors playing baseball.
Kyle had also spilled things,
dropped things,
and climbed and ravaged the cherry tree.

Dad himself had adjusted the car mirror
only to have it fall in his lap.
But I was, "The god damn kid
who could do nothing right."
I was the kid who wore the eye patch,
a handicapped fool.

Maple Syrup   ...March

We tapped the sugar maple trees today,
for fun, not profit.
Each tree with a spout—
like Pinocchio
with a pail hanging from his nose.

Grandma Swanson boiled
the liquid down
on her old, black,
coal-burning kitchen stove,
skimmed brown-skin foam
off the top,
and we feasted on limpa (Swedish bread),
and maple syrup.
Good!
Almost as good as candy.

Brad's Bike   ...April

Brad rode down on his bike today,
his blue, thin, sleek bike,
a *pre-fabricated* WW II bike,
purchased when men were soldiers,
and America was right!

We—Karl, Mitch, Brad, and I—
played basketball against the side of the barn
and baseball down in the field,
the air so cold,
our hands rattled with bumblebees
every time we hit the ball.

As usual, we played longer than intended,
and when Brad realized the time,
he hopped on his slick bike
and pedaled for home
as fast as his legs would churn.

For a minute!

Crossing the grass
in front of our house,
he flew up the mound
near the mailbox,
jumped the crest,
and pumped his legs as fast
as wheels on a locomotive.

"CRACK" snapped the bike
collapsing like a heap of rubble,
the pedals on the ground,
the bike weld's broken,
the wheels freely spinning on their sprockets.

The bike looked as if
someone had grabbed the front and back wheels
and bent them up and back
until they almost met,
Brad between them.

There was Brad
still sitting on the bike seat,
trying to pump the pedals
with his piston-like legs.

When he realized what had happened,
Brad started to wail
in wild frustration.

We thought it was the funniest thing,
Brad's bike sitting there,
Brad pumping his legs,
the wheels spinning,

the bike a broken reminder of what had been.

The more we laughed,
the more Brad,
like Rumpelstiltsken,
ranted and raved,
angry at his broken bike,
enraged that his best friends
had laughed at him.

We shouldn't have laughed,
we knew that,
but who can stop three boys,
when the sight is right,
and the time is now?

The Poor Bumble Bee   ...April

The plump, pollen-laden bumblebee

        zipped and zapped,

            zapped and zipped,

from hollyhock to hollyhock.

I caught him unaware,
as I had snagged others before,
and caged him
pinching the hollyhock closed.

He didn't like it one bit,
angrily buzzed,
and malevolently stung my thumb.

For all his buzzing and stinging,
he gave his all,
a broken husk beneath my shoe.

I regretted my retaliation.

He was the victim, not I.
Albert Schweitzer
would have been kinder,
more forgiving.

I covered my throbbing thumb
with mud
and chided myself—
that busy bumblebee,
some beetle's breakfast.

Poison Ivy, Poison Sumac   ...April

Aunt Marion laughed
and told
how when she was a child,
Grandpa and Grandma Swanson,
held her
and scrubbed her poison ivy blisters
raw
with a hard brush
and then
poured alcohol on her oozing flesh
to make her heal.

"I'd rather have the poison ivy," I thought,
"I'm the one who gets poison ivy now,"
as I felt her pain and shuttered.
Grandma and Grandpa meant well,
but meaning well
didn't lessen Aunt Marion's torture.

Another cousin
ate poison sumac.

It almost killed him,
his throat swelling up
so he couldn't breathe.

Which would be worse?
Breath-taking poison sumac
or blister-brushed poison ivy?

I only know that when I was eight,
poison ivy covered my privates
so badly
with pus and blisters
I knew Mom would
take me to Dr. Payne
if I told her.

And I couldn't show Mom.
I'd have been too embarrassed,
so I showed my teenage cousin, Barbara
taking her into Grandpa's woodshed.

When Barbara saw the oozing,
pus-covered blisters,
she went cross-eyed,
said I'd get infected,
and told my Mom.

Mom took me to Dr. Payne.

Hiking in the Woods   ...April

We—Kyle, Karl and I—
walked with Mom towards Hart's Mountain.

She loved those walks
and pointed

                    to this and that

                              here and there.

"There's a pissybed,"
(her name for them, not mine.)
"There's some white and purple violets."
"And there's the season's first jack-in-the-pulpit."

"Over there...
over there is a lady slipper."

And Kyle yelled,
"Over on that rock

under those birch
is a copperhead sunning!"

Later,
I saw and wanted to say,
"Over there! In that tire track,
a Four Roses bottle!
Dad was here before us!"

Bloody Curtains   ...April

Grandma washed
the living room and dining room curtains today.
I tried to be helpful
and hung the white, shear curtains
on the curtain stretcher
I had assembled earlier on the porch.

Stretching and hanging curtains was no fun,
the little, sharp pins pricked my fingers.
Finally, Grandma said in exasperation,
"Go out and play, Kurt.
Find something else to do.
You are getting blood all over my clean, white curtains."

Mom   ...April

Mom, our breadwinner,
is over-worked and underpaid.

I don't understand how
she keeps going day after day
up all night,
night after night,
with our demanding Dad.

Mom is an accountant
for a firm in New Britain,
a CPA,
a Certified Public Accountant
with only eight years of schooling.

Karl and I have as much education,
and Kyle more.

She has such perfect handwriting
and mine so bad!

From January to March
during the tax season,
Mom hauled her adding machine home
and worked on the dining room table
at nights
and on the weekends.

Her clients brought her
candy or flowers as extra favors
to get their taxes done
by the Ides of March.[1]

Dad is fifty-five,
and Mom is forty-three,
but older than her age.

I wondered
if she knew
what she was getting into
when she married Dad.

Was he, at forty,
when they married,
already on his downhill slide?

I suspected so,
but Mom didn't talk about it,
a reticent, closed-mouthed Yankee.

---

[1]In 1948, Income taxes were due March 15

Kyle was born in '33.
Karl and I, were born in '35,
fraternal twins,
early arrivals,
three months premature,
incubator twins for six months.
For SIX MONTHS!
Karl and I
the runts of the litter!

We were lucky to survive
back then when the risks
were far, far greater.

Karl and I will be thirteen in June.

Last month we helped
our short, non-complaining Mom,
shovel out her '41 Chevy,
scraped the windows,
and put the snow chains on
her fading blue car
so she could
         cautiously,
                  nervously
drive the seven miles to New Britain
afraid her pay would be docked
if she didn't get there before 8 a.m.

Did I mention that Mom's an accountant,
A CPA,
with only an eighth grade education?

We had heard the tales
of how she,
or one of her six brothers and sisters,
used to hitch up the buggy
on wintry days
and take Grandpa to work
at Stanley Works,
and repeat the trip each afternoon.

There are a lot of questions
I'd like to ask sometime.
But Mom is Mom,
and some things
she'd talk about,
and some things not!

Why did Mom marry Dad?
For all his legendary greatness,
she could,
I think,
have made a better choice.

But then,
Karl and I
and Kyle,
would not be here,
so I'll not complain too much
this time!

But I think
"What Might Have Been"
if we had had a different father,
a loving, caring father
who patiently taught us

how to ride a bike,

to camp and swim,

to bunt and hit and run,

and to help us do our homework.

Would I be a better student?
A less nervous youngster?
A gifted athlete?

Maybe so.

But for all my wishful thinking,
I'm stuck with my nightmares
and Dad's,
"Get me another god damn drink,"
and "Can't you do anything right?"

How did Mom put up with him?
When did she get her sleep,
her traipsing down the upstairs hall
at midnight,
at one and two,
fetching for him,
as he lay in bed,
in his shorts,
his Four Roses
when she worked
so hard each day?

And why?

Please why?
Tell me why she gave him money
or bought him booze.

It was hard enough
to raise three rambunctious kids
much less a drunkard husband.

I saw her, too,
slipping the food and rent money
into Grandma's cupboard,
thirty dollars
twice a month.

One thing surprised me,
Dad being the way he was.
Mom liked her Christmas eggnog
spiked,
generously spiked.

I don't know what I'd think or do
if she got sick,
if she got drunk.

Just thinking about it
made me nervous.

Still, she was my Mom
               underpaid,
                    overworked,
                           and undervalued.

Mom,
I love you
even if I cannot tell you—
old Yankee Show-No-Affection
so ingrained by you and Dad.

Lucky Bum!   ...April

Karl and I went fishing at Hartland Lake today.

I, the one who fishes the most,
had little luck,
but Karl caught,
on a red and white spoon,
a huge pickerel,
two feet long
and three pounds—
or more—
the biggest fish we've ever caught,
and I,
old Kurt,
filled with envy,
cried,
"Karl, you were just a lucky bum!"

Ouch!   ...April

A cousin who lives in Bristol
was helping his mother
wash the clothes
and his arm was pulled
into the washer wringer.

He'll be OK,
no bones crushed or broken,
but may have a permanent scar
once the terrible pain
goes away.

My Cousin's Bike   ...April

Today I thought about the bike
I had borrowed
from my cousin Barbara
who lives across the street.

I raced down High Hill Road
fast as a pursued rabbit,
and rode "no hands,"
the wind blowing in my face,
king of High Hill Road
until I hit a pot hole
and flew off the bike
and landed butt-over-elbow,
the handlebars twisted
but not broken,
the back fender bent,
but fixable,
my blue jeans torn,
my knee badly gouged and bleeding,
the same for the palm of my right hand,
my head throbbing, my eyelid swelling.

"Mom will kill me if she finds out," I thought,
knowing she'll be more concerned
about Barbara's bike than my cuts and bruises.

And she was.

"Bring Barbara's bike back
after you fix it.
Apologize, and offer to pay
if need be."

I fixed Barbara's bike,
cleaned up, bandaged up,
and returned the bike as good as when I got it.

Barbara wasn't home
and wouldn't have cared.
She's eighteen, and dating.

I told Uncle Fritz.

He laughed and laughed,
then asked,
"Didn't your mother, Aunt Ellen,
tell you that you have a magnificent shiner?"

Escape to Freedom   ...May

Kyle, Karl, and I,
condemned criminals,
Sunday School our punishment,
Miss Grace, our bespeckled teacher,
well-meaning,
sincere,
knew no humor.

At ten, we escaped,
and fled down Pac's Hill

    zigzagging through the woods

        hurtling smooth boulders and rotten stumps,

            shouting,

                running,

                    jumping,

                        racing!

We reached the double bridge,
Kyle in the lead,
halfway home.

"We were free.
Free! Free! Free!"

We had slipped
the coiled, dangling noose,
free as dandelion fluff
on a windy day.

Trout Fishing   ...May

Today Brad and I
went trout fishing in the brook
at the bottom of the long hill
that slopes from his wood-surrounded home.

Brad was kind
and lent me his father's,
our Scoutmaster's,
trout equipment,
a big mistake!

Brad snagged one nice
"Brookie,"
and then,
as I awkwardly cast the line,
the tip of my borrowed fly rod
caught an overhanging branch
and the slim, sleek rod snapped in two.

Brad's father was gracious
when I anxiously told him

the fate of his precious fly rod
and refused my offer to pay.

But I was mortified
and Brad was devastated.

He had not asked permission
to let me use and break his father's treasure.

(Later, Brad told me,
our beloved Scoutmaster
blistered the hide off his generous son
with non-Scout-like reprimands.)

Horse Chestnut Tree ...May

The horse chestnut tree
below the summer house
is in full bloom.

When the frost comes in October,
Karl and I will climb in it
and gather
the half-split-open horse chestnuts.

There was something about
a horse chestnut,
a Buckeye,
      its dark brown color,
           its round, uneven shape,
                its sensuous slickness...

I'm sure I'm was not the only one
who had a lucky horse chestnut
in his pocket.

Our old horse chestnut tree
was dying,
a blight attacking it.

Grandpa said
all the horse chestnut trees
would soon disappear,
destroyed by blight.

I hope he's wrong,
for once.

Nightmares   ...May

I have had terrifying nightmares
ever since I can remember.

Two of them repeated themselves
again and again.

I thought that if I knew what they meant,
they'd stop.

In the first,
I frantically ran
from classroom to classroom
trying to find my lost homework.

My teacher scolded me.
Mom nagged at me.

I asked for help
but no one would assist me.

And then I woke up
in a cold sweat,
   breathless,

        trembling,

            screaming.

The second was far worse.
I had it again last night.

I was alone
climbing a high,
barren mountain peak,
a lone cabin
balanced at the edge.

The wind started blowing,
black clouds swirled above the cabin,
and I frantically ran for cover.

The rain pounded down,
and I got soaked,
the cabin roofless.

Then the rain stopped,
the winds blew harder,
and as I looked up,
rocks and boulders
tumbled out of the clouds
           dropping,
                  falling,
                        plunging

toward my little cabin.

Faster and faster they fell,
big ones,
small one,
eager to crush me.

They kept falling and falling
barely missing me.

I knew they would
        smash me,
             flatten me
                  bloody me
as I lay in a corner
of that little cabin,
     soaked,
        shivering,
           breathless,
            terrified,
              whimpering,
until I woke up
in a cold sweat,
my heart pounding,
Mom saying,
"It's all right, Kurt,
you're having another nightmare."

I think those nightmares
had something to do with Dad!

But I just didn't know what.

Uncle Fritz   ...May

Uncle Fritz brought over a pot
of snapping turtle soup last night.
Thank goodness,
Mom didn't make us eat any.

I liked Uncle Fritz.
He was different!
But I didn't like it
when he delivered
those delicacies for us to taste.

He had brought us wild mushrooms,
venison,
frog legs,
and pigs feet.

Uncle Fritz fancied himself
the family doctor and
chef without peer.
(His baked beans were excellent!)

Mom laughed
and tried some of his offerings,
but not his wild mushrooms
which she suspected were poisonous.
Uncle Fritz, Mom's sister's husband,
could send Grandma Swanson
into a dither
faster than a telegram.

Our Uncle was fifty, or so,
and liked to dress casually
so casually,
he often dropped by
wearing summer shorts,
an undershirt,
or no shirt at all.

Grandma was from the old school,
and Uncle Fritz's bare arms
and hairy chest drove her daffy.

She didn't confront Uncle Fritz,
but after he crossed High Hill Road
and headed back home,
she'd say to us,
"My daughter, Stella—God bless her soul!—
married a man that has no shame."

We wouldn't tell Uncle Fritz,
our self-proclaimed family doctor,
that we had sore throats,
his cure worse than a root canal.
But Mom would tell,
and Uncle Fritz would hurry over,

with torture on his mind.

He'd have his *doctor's bag,*
filled with secret potions
and this and that,
and say, "Open wide,"
and paint our throats
with a concoction
worse than snake spit.

We were not sure what was in it,
but we thought it contained:
                cod liver oil
                     road tar,
                          paregoric,
                              and poison.

Whatever...it was the worst tasting stuff
a guy ever had to pass through his lips,
and as best we could tell
it made the patient sicker.

Mom might call him once,
if we are foolish enough
to complain of a sore throat,
but we won't complain twice!

Uncle Fritz's wife, Stella,
was the one I thought of
when I thought about Whalen Sauls,
our second grade classmate
who died with a brain tumor.

Aunt Stella died two years before Whalen did.
First she had a big lump
on the front of her forehead,
then she had an operation,
returned home,
bald,
and wore a white turban on her head.

A new lump appeared,pushed the bandage out,
and all too soon,
she died.

That was seven years ago.

Now, rumor has it,
that Uncle Fritz
has a woman friend,
a widow who works with him at the American Can Company.
but if it is so,
none of us have met her yet.

I hope the rumor is true.

Therapy   ...May

About once a month,
when Dad was feeling up to it,
he drove,
or Mom took him,
to get a massage,
"For therapy," he said,
from Dr. Marshall,
the Chiropractor.

Dr. Marshall's office,
behind a big, gray, weather-worn fence,
was a mysterious,
forbidding place.

Dad went willingly,
returned in an hour, or so,
and said he felt better.
                He didn't look better.
                    He didn't act better.
I kept waiting
to see improvements,
but I saw no signs of that.

Dad's Birthday   ...May

It was Dad's birthday yesterday,
a pitiful event.
He was fifty-six.
Mom took us shopping at the Five and Ten
the day before.

What do you get a Dad
when he was a Dad the shape he was in?
Cigarettes?
Four Roses?
New underwear?

Even worse
was having *a party*
for him in his bedroom,
him lying there
under the sheet,
face unshaven,
hair uncombed,
trying to *celebrate* his birthday.

Kyle got him a jackknife

so he could shave match sticks into toothpicks.
"That's wonderful Kyle,
just what I want and needed,
the best present ever."

Karl got him a coffee mug,
although he doesn't drink coffee.
"Good, Karl.
Mom can bring me milk in that."

Mom got him one of those new,
fancy ball-point pens
that just came out in the stores.

"That's just what I needed, Ellen"
he ooohs and aaahs,
"I'll do my crossword puzzles with it."

I gave him a paperback biography
about Jim Thorpe, the legendary football player.
"To DAD from Kurt"
although Dad never reads.

"Oh, Kurt," he said, "A book?"

Was that a compliment?

Memorial Day Parade   ...May

Today our Boy Scout Troop 5
marched in Blue Hill's
Memorial Day Parade.

What a motley crew we were,
rag-muffins,
some wearing Scout shirts and blue jeans,
some with white socks,
some with no uniform at all.

But still,
it was great fun,
marching in cadence
to the Legion's band,
children carrying
little "Old Glory" flags
to West Lane Cemetery,
the air cool,
the crowd proud,
the cemetery beautiful
with its wreaths, flowers and flags.

Dad, an honored veteran,asleep in bed.

Birthday Twins   …June

Karl and I are thirteen today.
The hoped for B-B guns
unclaimed in that hardware store.

But we are no longer boys
no matter what THEY say.
We'll join the church in September,
be baptized Congregationalists,
and choose our own middle names.
I'll be
Kurt *Swanson* Thomas
after my grandfather.

Karl will be
Karl *George* Thomas
after Dad.

George, a hateful name.
I would not have it.
Better to have no middle name
than that of my father!

Thomas was bad enough.

But no B-B guns today
nor last Christmas either!

New bikes
hidden behind the door
leading to the cellar
weren't half so bad.
(Why didn't we think
to look there!)

And I wondered
how Mom managed.

Grandma Swanson
gave us a dollar each,
smiled, and said,
"Happy birthday, Karl and Kurt!
Go get some ice cream
or whatever,
and I'll bake a blueberry pie for you, Kurt,
and a lemon meringue for you, Karl."

Another Fish Story ...June

Uncle Ed Swanson, Mitch's Dad,
took us to Hartland Lake
to fish for bluegills today.

We called them

    "bluegills,"

        "sunfish," and

            "Johnnie roaches."

He pushed his rowboat into the water,
and there never were
three more excited kids who loved to fish.

And God was with us.
I don't know why!

It was a once-in-a-blue-moon adventure.

Out in the boat, ten feet from shore,
we caught a bluegill
every cast,
Mitch, Karl, Uncle Ed, and I
pulling the eager,
hungry fish in faster than Dad could curse.

Within two hours,
we had a galvanized tub half filled
with bluegill, sunfish, Johnny roaches,
and a yellow perch or two.

What fun we had,
pulling in fish after fish,
often catching
two, three, and four fish
on the same worm.

When we got to Uncle Ed's house,
we had to clean them,
and that's no fun,
but Uncle Ed ended up doing most of the work,
his cleaning board bloody and fishy,
the air smelling of guts and scales.

Tonight, Grandma Swanson
fried our share of the breaded fish,
bluegill, sunfish, Johnny roaches, and perch
into golden, brown, crispy bites.

We have never had a better supper.

Grandpa, with his one leg,
loved them so,
and Karl and I
SO PROUD!

Uncle Ed   ...June

Uncle Ed is fashioning
a secret hiding place for Mitch,
a small alcove,
a private place
above the cellar,
below the kitchen,
a place where Mitch
can read his comic books,
and take his games.

I suspect he's building it
so Mitch can flee
from Aunt Edith's nerves.

Uncle Ed
always did the unexpected,
and drove an old '32 Plymouth
to work each day
just to hear what folks would say.

At home,
he raised golden pheasants,
rabbits, pigeons,and mink.

He raised them, I think,
to have an excuse
to hide from Aunt Edith.

Years ago,
he was a playful Gepetto,
and carved delicate, beautiful birds
which decorated
the knickknack shelves
in their spacious,
envious house,
a home he built
for his new, blushing bride,
Aunt Edith,
twenty years ago.

He also carved
fancy table stands
out of birch limbs—
artistic treasures, too.

And then there were
his tiny figurines of naked,
full-figured women,

        twirling,

           dancing,

              running.

Uncle Ed should have been an artist.

Aunt Edith
had seen the figurines,
but he kept them hidden,
because Aunt Edith condemned them,
"So disgusting!"

Uncle Ed showed them to us nonetheless,
and said with a mischievous smile,
"They make her nervous."

They, too, I thought,
were works of art,
intriguing,
if suggestive.

And on occasion,
Uncle Ed would let us peek
into his second cellar,
his dirt-floored cold cellar,
and show us
onions, potatoes, carrots,
and the dusty kegs
that held his homemade wine.

Uncle Ed would cross the street
to talk to Mom and Grandma,
and it made me sad
to hear him tell
how Aunt Edith
would not allow him
near her
anymore.

Kyle   ...June

Kyle isn't as bad as
I make him out to be—
tricking me
to freeze my lips on that pump, and all.

I've watched other older brothers,
and some are much worse.

Kyle will play a prank,
but there's nothing
hateful about him.

He's fifteen,
has different interests,
and is closed-mouth
just like Mom.

Dad's already encouraging Kyle
to start learning how to drive.
(Mom's not so keen,

but says little.)

Kyle's good looking,
and a capable first-string end on the football team.
(Go Redcoats!)

When he made a tackle
last fall,
he had a front tooth
knocked out!

There's no doubt, too,
that Kyle's everybody's favorite.
And that's OK.

Still,
I wish he'd let us use
or give us
his B-B gun.

He doesn't know
and see the same Dad I see,
and that bothers me—
not that we don't see eye to eye—
but it makes me wonder,
if he is right,
or me.

There are probably a lot of things
about Dad
I haven't seen or heard.

I guess
I not only had to wear that eye patch,
but that I've still got blinders on
when it comes to Dad.

When Kyle had his paper route,
Dad would say,
"Kyle's the best paper boy
there ever was."

Or, when he was able
to see one football game,
Dad bragged,
"I think of how I played
at Rockwell College
when I see Kyle out there
making those tremendous tackles."

Kyle's chest swelled, of course.
and so would mine,
if Dad could find something
to brag on me about.
Kyle isn't going to give
Karl and me his B-B gun,
that's for sure,
but nonetheless
I guess I'll keep my older brother
until I can find a better one.

Grandma Thomas Is Sick   ...June

We heard today that Grandma Thomas is sick.
Nothing serious.
Mom went to see her.
"A touch of pneumonia," Mom said.

We liked Grandma Thomas well enough,
but she was not our favorite grandmother.

Grandpa Thomas loves her,
and she thinks George, her son, my Dad,
is God's gift to mankind,
and favors him over Uncle Kurt—
Uncle Kurt, always sober,
also a veteran,
and the drum major
of New Britain's Legionnaire band.

Mom and Grandma Thomas get along OK,
but have little to say to each other.
I don't know that Grandma has much to say to anyone.

She's no cook!
She sure can ruin good sauerkraut!

Brave Aunt Edith   ...June

Aunt Edith was going down the back steps
yesterday morning
to feed Uncle Ed's animals,
and when she looked down,
she saw a large copperhead
lounging in a corner of the step,
sunbathing.

Aunt Edith said,
"I let out a shriek,
but no one was there to help me,
so I ran back up the stairs,
raced to the cellar,
got a hoe,
and chopped that snake to pieces."

I would have given a dollar
to see that,
Aunt Edith
our nervous heroine!

Grandma Thomas Dies …June

Grandma Thomas died three days ago.
The funeral was today
at Benson's funeral home in New Britain.

Grandpa Thomas, of course,
was bent and heartbroken,
her death so sudden, so unexpected.
"Pneumonia," the doctors repeated.

Mom, Kyle, Karl, and I
sat next to Grandpa in the funeral home.

Dad couldn't make it,
he was too sick,
of course.

To be honest, we three boys,
each in our best suits,
were indifferent.
We liked Grandma,

but not nearly so much as Grandma Swanson.
We loved Grandma Swanson.
Kyle, maybe,
loved Grandma Thomas, but…
Well, I just don't know.

We felt sad for Grandpa,
Grandma's death so unexpected.

After the service
we proudly rode with Grandpa out to the cemetery
in a big, dark green limousine.

Traffic stopped for us,
and a string of cars
three blocks long
trailed behind,
Grandma's coffin in a dark green hearse
leading the "parade."

It was hot and humid at the cemetery.
Grandma was buried under a big maple.
I hope she liked that.

The minister threw a handful of dirt on the coffin,
and Grandpa cried.
So did Uncle Kurt.
Mom's eyes got red.

After the burial,
we rode back in the limousine
to a cousin's house
and ate cookies, ice cream, and drank soda pops

provided by friends and neighbors.

All we wanted!
Everybody laughed and joked
and told stories about a Grandma we don't know.

Karl and I went outside,
found a well-worn tennis ball,
and played catch.

Happy Birthday, Mom   ...June

It was Mom's birthday today.
She's forty-four.

Grandma baked Mom a spice cake,
and Aunt Marion, Aunt Edith,
and Uncle Fritz came by for dessert.

Mom's birthday was a sad little event,
but Mom seemed to appreciate it.

I guess when you are that old,
birthdays are no fun anymore.

We didn't see hide nor hair of Dad.
He hasn't been out of the house,
so if he gave her a present,
it must have been
a bottle of Four Roses
and a night of peaceful sleep.

Last Day of School   ...June

Yesterday was the last day of school.
I don't mind school,
but I sure like summer vacation better
even with the chores:
mowing the lawn,
cleaning the chicken coop,
gathering wood,
and hoeing and weeding the garden.

In September,
we'll go to Blue Hills High,
and I'm going to try out for the football team.
We'll also go to classes,
passing from room to room,
eat in the cafeteria,
and start school earlier
and get home earlier, too.

There'll be barn dances,
pep rallies,
and football, basketball, and baseball games.

Here I am wishing high school would begin
and the first day of vacation
hasn't started yet.

An Angel Visits   ...June

Last night well past midnight,
I woke up
after Dad stopped crying out
and there—
standing on the floor near my bed
radiating light—
was the tiniest angel ever,
bent over
silently praying.

She scared the daylights out of me.

I thought it was my Aunt Stella,
long dead with a brain tumor,
visiting from Heaven.

I wanted to call my mom,
but held my tongue,
not wanting to look
perfectly stupid.

Some part of me
knew it wasn't an angel…
another, that it was.

I lay there looking at her
waiting for that miniature angel

                to move,

                        to speak,

                                to ascend.

I must have lain there five minutes
or more,
and when I finally found the courage
to turn on the light,
Aunt Stella,
the littlest, glowing angel,
turned into a carelessly dropped handkerchief
edged by moonlight
streaming through the window.

Fourth of July

A good day.
We exploded the few firecrackers we had,
and then our second cousin, Brad, from Hartland Hill
came down,
with tons of rockets, torpedoes, and cherry bombs.

We "blew up" toy soldiers,
ant hills,
and even dropped them in milk cans
to make them sound like booming cannons.

This evening,
Mitch, Karl, and I,
walked the mile plus
to Brad's house,
and his Dad,
our Scoutmaster,
an architect,
put on his annual Fourth of July display.

It was magnificent.

All their neighbors were there,
sitting on folding chairs
or blankets.
Brad and his father
lit
    Roman candles,
        pinwheels,
            star bursts,
                and giant rockets
as fast as they could,
the rockets blasting high into the dark sky
cascading bright reds, yellows, and blues
back toward the crowds,
"Ooohs," and "aaaahs," answering each.

Later,
after we walked home in the dark,
past the scary West Lane Cemetery,
and reached the safety of Grandma's house,
I remembered Mr. Josephowitcz's new barn,
the Polish farmer whose whiskey cache,
we had found and broken
near the cemetery in March.

Fourth of July a year ago,
it was early afternoon,
Karl, Mitch, Brad, and I
were playing as we usually do,
after we had spent all our fireworks,
when Mitch yelled,
"I smell smoke!"

We ran around the side of the barn,

and there across the field,
about three football fields away,
on Chamberlain Highway,
we saw the black, billowing smoke,
and the hateful flames
rolling and blasting into the air
thirty feet or more,
Mr. Josephowitcz's barn in total flames.

As we raced across the field,
we heard the distant fire siren.

We got there
the same time that the fire truck
and the volunteers in their private cars and trucks
raced up,
their gravel-grabbing tires screeching to a halt.

But it was too late,
The firemen couldn't save the new barn,
but, at least,
Mr. Josephowitcz's two cows
and his work horse
had been led to the pasture.

By the time the firemen drove away,
all that was left
were smoldering, charged bits of beams,
and a sad, soiled
immigrant farmer
wearing mucking boots
standing beside them.

"Boy, now that is what I call fireworks!"

I said as we slowly crossed the field
and went back home.
But my heart wasn't in it.

Poor Mr. Josephowitcz.

Best Birthday Ever   ...July

For Kyle's fifteenth birthday,
Mom took a vacation day
and drove Kyle, Karl, and me
to Lake Congomond
and Babb's Amusement Park.

What a time we had!

We saw Chanticleer,
the big rooster
we always look for,
grandly guarding someone's farm.

We even took an hour
to descend into the cave
at Old Newgate Prison
where Confederate weapons
and soldiers
were kept,
the prisoners shackled
to the wall
beaten and tortured.

Then we saw the miles and miles
of white tobacco tents,
fields of canvas-covered snow.

At Babb's,
we swam,
and dove into the cool lake
from the huge waterwheel,
and off the diving board
out on the raft.

For lunch we ate
foot-long hotdogs
with sweet green relish
and just a touch of yellow mustard
and washed them down
with icy, birch beer soda.

Then there was the bumping cars,
skating in the big, blaring roller rink,
and playing Skee-Ball games.

Kyle won a pair of dice
to decorate his bedroom wall.

Karl won an ID braceletwhich will soon turn black on his wrist.

And I, a big, orange yo-yo,
its string already broken!

But what fun.

Then we stopped
at Dad's Aunt Lucy's cottage
at the edge of Lake Congomond,
said, "Hello,"
and petted her cats,
dozens and dozens of cats
while Mom and Aunt Lucy jabbered.

Dad's aunt's cottage smelled so—
cat fur, and cat urine—
we were glad when Mom nodded,
and said, "Time to go, boys."

Then past home, on to the Italian Restaurant
in Meriden,
where we gorged on Vertolini's pizza.

The end of an almost perfect day,
we thought. But when we got home,
Mom pulled presents out of her closet,
and Kyle got school clothes,
two books—
and I can't believe it—
a new, repeating, pellet gun!

I don't know what Dad did all day.
Slept, I guess,
wondering who would bring
his boloney sandwich.

It wasn't me.
It wasn't Karl.

It wasn't the Birthday Boy,
the do-no-wrong,
the new-pellet-gun-owner, Kyle.

I'm sure Mom had made Dad's sandwich
and put it on his table
before we left.

Grandma and Grandpa Swanson
never, never, never,
went upstairs when Dad was home,
and now that Grandpa was getting worse,
and has but one leg,
he certainly couldn't, wouldn't have climbed the stairs.

Grandma said,
of course,
"Kyle, here's a dollar,
go get some ice cream tomorrow,
or whatever,
and I'll bake you
a blueberry pie!"

Before the day ended,
Kyle kissed Mom,
and said,
"Thanks, Mom,
that was the best birthday ever!"
And if Kyle had given us

his old, worn B-B gun,
his Red Ryder,
it would have been.

Another Fire   ...July

Mr. Josephowitcz's barn fire reminded me of the time
the big three-ring tent caught on fire,
the day cousin Mitch and Aunt Edith
went to Hartford to see the Barnum and Bailey Circus.

Karl and I were so envious
we could taste our own green jealousy.

We had hoped Aunt Edith
would take us with them,
but no invitations came
(not that we did hint for them!).

When Mitch and Aunt Edith climbed in the car
and headed to the train station,
we knew there was no hope!
To the circus
and by train, too!

Mitch was the luckiest guy alive.

To hide our hurt and disappointment,
after lunch,
Karl and I put on our bathing suits,grabbed our towels,
and headed to the Double Bridge
to go swimming.

Walking home,
we watched the heat mirages on the tar road
appear and disappear,
and told each other what a great time
Mitch had had at the
Greatest Show on Earth.

We pictured jostling, gay clowns
climbing out of miniature autos,
horses galloping around the ring,
fearless riders standing on the horses' backs,
and braver men
running across thin wires
a million miles up in the sky.

"There's been a fire,"
Grandma Swanson cried
when we casually walked in the door late that afternoon,
"at the circus in Hartford.
We don't know the details,
but many people have been hurt and killed!
We haven't heard about Aunt Edith and Mitch!"

We waited and waited for a report,
wondering and fearing
if they had been burned
or killed.

That evening,
we gratefully learned
that they had escaped,
unharmed!
But Grandma's two half-brothers,
who lived in New Britain,
had been badly burned,
and one might die.

Later,
after both recovered,
one badly scarred,
we learned their story.

The older brother, Harold,
had helped lower his brother, Robert,
through the flames that licked at them,
and before the older
could jump,
he himself was shrouded with flames
his body cooked.

"It's only a miracle my brother is alive,"
Robert said, sounding guilty,
when they finally visited Grandma Swanson.
"If Harold hadn't helped me,
we might both have died."

It's funny,
Mitch doesn't talk about that circus fire.

I'd like to ask him about it some time.
I know I won't,
but if Mitch should talk about it,
I'll ask my questions:
"Where did the fire start?"
"How close to it were you?"
"Did Aunt Edith panic?"
"How about you, Mitch?
"How frightened were you?"
"How bad was the smoke?"
"How did you get out?"

And more importantly
"WHY DIDN'T YOU TAKE US WITH YOU?"

Homemade Root Beer   ...July

Grandma Swanson made homemade root beer in the kitchen.
We helped.
We went to the cellar and got the large and small,
dusty, dark green antique bottles.

Grandma washed them,
and got the huge kettle
she used for canning
and put it on the black coal stove.

We filled the kettle with water,
and as the water warmed,
(she wouldn't let it get hot),
Grandma added root beer extract,
yeast dissolved in a cup of water,
and tons of sugar
and stirred til everything dissolved.

Then came the fun.
Using a pitcher and a shiny tin funnel,
one of us filled each bottle,
and another pressed the bottle caps

with the old bottle capper,pushing the handle down
until the cap "clicked" tight.

We took turns.

When the job was done,
we loaded ten, fifteen, twenty bottles,
or more,
into bushel baskets
and lined them out in the sun
near Mom's flower garden
to let the yeast start working.

After the sun set,
we gently carried the bottles in.

Some went in the refrigerator,
some went on shelves in the pantry,
and some went into the dark, dusty cellar.

One we opened
and drank the warm, flat root beer
a hint of the "good stuff"
we would claim in three or four days.

Chores   ...July

I can't remember when
we didn't have chores to do,
even more
when Grandpa was well.

Today I weeded the small garden
Grandpa insisted we plant last spring.
Then I plucked potato bugs.

As I worked,
I heard—
when the wind was right—
the joyful calls and cries
from the town's baseball field,
and wished I were chasing fly balls
and grounders
rather than squashing
                    fat,
                        greedy
                            potato bugs.

Last week
I cleaned the chicken coop, scraping chicken manure
with a hoe
into piles
and then shoveling it
into the wheelbarrow
and spreading it
on Grandpa's garden.

I'll admit I didn't dislike the work,
the coop looking so much better,
and Grandma's dime,
and then she'd fill her galvanized tub
with hot water heated on the stove
so I could take a bath
to rid myself of chicken mites.

Grandma's Cooking   ...July

Grandma Swanson was an excellent Swedish cook,
her Christmas corve, lutfisk, headcheese, pult, frut supa,
and silla patatees
favored by her Swedish relatives.

Corve is a Swedish sausage,
Lutfisk, a smelly, smoked, dried cod
re-constituted with water,
and served with a white, gravy-like sauce.
Pult is pig blood mixed with flour, seasoned,
and baked into thick, loaf-like bread.
Headcheese is a congealed pig head gelatin.
Silla patatees or sill and potatoes, a stew-like mix.
Frut supa, a fruit soup, as best I know,
with prunes, apricots, tapioca, and raisins
cooked with cinnamon sticks,
cloves and mounds of sugar.

Most dishes
better tasting than they sounded
although I turned my nose up at some,
the smell overwhelming.

Grandma is good with other food, too,
her pies and pastries, envied, tasty morsels:
blueberry, lemon meringue, peach, apple, and raisin.

But she was matchless
cooking red meat.

She fried hamburger, steaks, lamb and pork chops,
extra long,
"to kill the terroristic trichinosis!"
and each burger and chop
metamorphosed
into a tasteless coal of cinder.

Grandma Swanson's Birthday   ...July

Grandma was seventy-five yesterday.

Because Dad is at the VA again,
Mom was able to take Grandma
and us to Vertolini's in Meriden
for Grandma's birthday dinner.
Our three-score-ten-and five
thoroughly Swedish Grandma,
loved Italian pizza
with pepperoni.

She tried some meatballs and spaghetti,
and had a glass of wine.

We gave her our modest presents:
        handkerchiefs,
                    scarves,
                            and more handkerchiefs,
and she paid for the meal.

"Happy Birthday, Grandma!"

Dad Looks Better   ...July

Dad has been in the VA
for the past two weeks.

He looks some better,
but Mom
not so sure,
I guess,
because she doesn't say
and there's that look about her.

Well, at least
it will be quiet a few more days.
Every day counts...
I mean every night counts.

Father Murphy Pulls Our Legs   ...July

Last Sunday afternoon
at the VA,
Father Murphy told us
how he lost his leg:

You do know, Kyle, Kurt, and Karl
that I've one pretty good leg
and a wooden one?

You see, boys, he continued,
as you know,
I was a Chaplain
during WW I,
and when I wasn't with my men
and praying,
hunting extra food,
composing letters for those who
couldn't write,
I was writing to those parents
who had lost another son.

Back then,
you see, lads, back then
they couldn't recruit enough chaplains
so I volunteered with my wooden leg,
and all.

They were hard up
for chaplains, I guess.

They not only took me,
they asked me if I
had any cousins
with a leg missing,
or two,
the good chaplain added with a laugh.

No, boys,
the truth be known,
I lost my leg
to a drunken surgeon.

It happened like this, lads.
I found a lot of eggs,
a mess of fresh, white eggs
in an shell-torn barn
right on that blasted battlefield, and knowing how hard
those surgeons
cut and sawed,
sawed and cut,
I figured they'd appreciate
a few fresh eggs for supper.
"Says, fellows,"
I says to those surgeons—
not realizing,

I'm afraid,
that they had had a little
too much sauce,
"You want some eggs?"

Well, boys,
one of the biggest
and toughest
grabbed me,
and before I could say "Sauerkraut,"
he tied me down,
and whacked my leg off
right at the knee.

I'll tell you, boys,that was no fun
and made me more than a little peeved.

I says to him,
I says,
"Doc, why'd you do that for?
Why'd you take my best leg?"

And that Doc
he answers right back,
"You told me to.
You asked me
'Do you want my leg?'"

And with that,
the good Father Murphy
roared again.

And then the playful chaplain continued:
Well, that surgeon
as surgeons go—
he weren't a bad sort
when he weren't drinking—
he said,
"Chaplain Murphy, old friend,
what can I do
to make my carving up to you,
I mean
whacking off your best leg and all?"

I thought about it rather carefully,
and I says,
"Doc, you could get me
another leg
if you were so inclined.
It ain't easy being a Chaplain,
prayin', hoppin', and runnin'
on my one leg
that ain't my best leg."

And so,
you know what that good Doc
and his buddies did?
They found an old birch branch
and carved out
the best leg you ever saw."

And then Chaplain Murphy
laughed again,
rolled up his uniformed trouser leg
and showed us his artificial leg
which we discovered
hadn't been carved

from a birch tree at all.

Then Father Murphy covered his leg
and said,
You know I got to be going, boys.
I've got others waiting for a story,
and quietly added,
I don't know about your Dad.
He's not doing quite so well.
I'm praying for him.
God bless you, lads,
and he shook our hands,
turned toward the VA Hospital
and limped away.

Thunderstorms   ...August

I loved to sit on the glider
on Grandma's porch
and watch
thunderstorms
roll in
day or night.

The sky would get darker,
the clouds meaner,
racing toward me,
racing menacingly,
and I'd count,
"One-thousand-one, one-thousand-two"
after I saw some lightning
to try to figure when the first rain
would reach the porch.

I had my nightmares,
but thunder and lightning
weren't their cause
unless I was out camping in them.

Night storms were even better,
the lightning flashing across the whole sky
revealing Grandma's porch,
night thunder sounding louder
than day thunder as it got
closer and closer.

I loved to watch those storms.

We had another last night,
imitating fireworks never lit
and fury never felt.

To the Tower   ...August

Five of us Troop 5 Boy Scouts—
Mitch, Brad, Cobb, Karl, and I—
hiked the seven miles
to Meriden Tower today.

It was a hike we took two or three
times a year
mindful of the traffic
along Chamberlain Highway,
taking side roads
when we could.

We hiked, and romped,
and joked and sang,
me, too,
even if I sang off key.

We loved to climb inside
the thin, stone Meriden Tower
to look at the city below,

to see creeks, steams, and ponds
where we didn't expect them,
the green hills looking bluish-green in the haze.

On the way home,
we stopped at Cumchick's,
the little hotdog stand
near the Meriden-Blue Hills town line
and bought foot-long hotdogs,
and ice cold root beer,
my hotdogs covered
with yellow mustard
and sweet green relish,
of course.

Another good day,
a day it seemed to me
perfect for guys
who will soon be busy freshmen.

Dad Gets Lunch   ...August

Dad, home again,
cried out most of the night
keeping us awake til
two or three
when only owls
and skunks might stir.

At noon I carried his lunch to him,
as Mom commanded—
Mom at work.

A hateful job.
I'd pay if Kyle or Karl
were so inclined
to do the dirty deed for me.

I took
a baloney sandwich,
an apple,
and a glass of milk

up the stairs on a tray,
hoped I wouldn't spill it,
and prayed that the old reveler
would be fast asleep.

No luck!

Dad was lying in bed,
unshaven,
wearing only dingy boxer shorts,
his body a white skeleton,
his hair a-tangle.

I spoke not.

There was nothing I could say,
and he had nothing to say to me,
the clumsy god damn bookworm
and imperfect athlete.

An apology would have been nice.
To Mom.
To Kyle, Karl, and me.
To Grandma and Grandpa
who, downstairs,
must have heard his demands
again last night.

"Ellen, I need a drink.
Ellen, I said, get me a god damn drink!"

Of course,
he swore and took the Lord's name
in vain,
his beverage of choice,
Four Roses.

He looked like
the rose of death.
I could have almost
felt sorry for him,
our World War I hero,
if I didn't dislike him so.

I fled.

Mom would ask me how he was.

"Fine," I'd say,
knowing it was not true.
And think:
"I wish I were old enough,

              and big enough,

                        and brave enough

to tell him
what I thought of him."

Some Better   ...August

It was my turn to take lunch
up to Dad
again.
To my surprise,
he looked some better,
and even thanked me
for the sandwich.

Years ago,
we loved to hear him tell
how he and a friend
went camping
and canoeing
when he was a late teen,
portaging their canoe
from lake to stream to lake,
                 paddling,
                     swimming,
                        cooking over an open fire
muskies and trout
snatched from rushing streams
and geese-seeking ponds.
It was

189

from the way Dad tells it,
a magic time for him.

His telling
was a magic time for us, too.

We dreamed
our own golden dreams
of canoeing across northern Minnesota
and southern Canada.

Finished   ...August 6

Dad died Saturday morning,

I, for one, had no idea!

I felt guilty.

Dad, home again after drying out,
seemed to be doing a little better,
and had not cursed me out
since May.

I couldn't believe it.
The day before I had brought him lunch,
and he seemed to be doing better.

Karl had mowed the lawn,
and I had weeded the garden,
and we were playing
a heated game of baseball
with Mitch and Brad

down in the field behind Grandpa's barn.
The score was 12 to 3,
Mitch and Karl
"whooping" Brad and me.

We were at bat,
well, Brad was,
when we heard Mom call,
"Boys, come here.
Come quick!"

"One more bat, Mom!" I called.
Karl yelled, "Brad, watch out for my wicked curve,"
and we laughed.

Karl's curve was as wicked
as a kitten sleeping on a window sill.

"Boys, come now," Mom cried,
"Come here,
NOW!"

Reluctantly, we headed up the hill,
and then raced
because we always raced.

Mom's eyes were red.

"Karl, Kurt,
I just found your Dad
DEAD.
He died in his bed, sleeping.

I found him just now,
when I got home from work."

"DEAD!"

If anything,
he looked a little better!

DAD IS DEAD.

"Brad, Mitch,
run home and tell your parents.
Karl, Kurt, go to the summer house
and wait with Kyle
until the doctor
and the undertaker come."

We do as she commands.

In the summer house,
I wondered
why the doctor has to come,
and Kyle told us,
"To confirm Dad's death,
and to sign the death certificate."
Kyle silently cried.
Karl, like I, felt bad,
but there were no tears from me.

Mixed with sadness for Mom
was ELATION!

"Dad is dead!" I thought.
"Who would believe it?
He looked better!
There will be no more nights
of fitful nightmares
and endless sleep!"

No more, "Get me another
god damn drink, Ellen!"

Saturday afternoon and evening,
and Sunday,
friends and relatives
came by,
brought food,
hugged Mom,
and told us,over and over,
"You Kyle, Kurt, and Karl
will have to be the men of the family now."

Monday,
Aunt Marion took us to New Britain
on the city bus,
to buy us news suits,
shirts, ties,
and shoes,
and at the shoe store
we looked into the X-ray machine
and watched our fluorescent toes
wiggling in our new shoes.

Tuesday evening,
we sat in Benson's Funeral Home

in our new suits
with Mom, Aunt Marion, Aunt Edith,
as our relatives and friends came by again,
hugged Mom,
cried,
and said,
"You Kyle, Kurt, and Karl
will have to be the men of the family now."

Today we buried Dad
down at West Lane Cemetery,
and I thought how we broke
Old Man Josephowitcz's whiskey bottles,
and remembered how Mom,
grief-stricken,
bent over Dad's coffin
at Benson's funeral home,
and kissed her wax-like husband,
our Dad,
on his painted, unreal, ripe-red lips.

"She loved him so," I think,
and wanted to cry for her,
disgusted because she could kiss that man,
her husband,
my father,
knowing I could not,
I would not,
if faced with death myself.

I felt badly,
confused,
angry at myself
that I was glad
that Dad had died!

I Forgot...   ...August

I forgot to tell
that at West Lane Cemetery
(with Grandpa home with his one leg),
how our poor old Grandma Swanson
who, sitting beside Dad's open grave
on a straw-caned chair,
leaned back,
and fell backwards
head over heels
next to Dad's gray coffin,
her bloomers showing.

To the Dump ...August

Mom stayed home a few days
after Dad died,
and today
we cleaned out Dad's bedroom.

What a mess!
I couldn't believe it!
His closet was packed
with empty Four Roses bottles
hidden there by Mom,
I suppose,
so Grandma and Grandpa
and we three kids
wouldn't find them.

If that wasn't surprise enough,
there were more empty bottles
stored in the attic
over his room—
bags and boxes,
scores and scores more!

I don't know how Mom got them in the attic.
There were no pull-down stairs.

We had to get the stepladder
from out into the garage
to haul them down.

We didn't even know there was an opening
that led to the attic in that closet,
and even Kyle admitted
he was "dumb" for not knowing.

Early in the morning,
Uncle Ed had taken
Grandma and Grandpa
to the hospital
so Grandpa Swanson
could have more tests.

Mom says, "Things don't look promising
for Grandpa Swanson right now."

We had the house to ourselves,
well planned, by Mom, I know.

We got bushel baskets from the basement
and took load after load in a wheelbarrow down
to the dump near The Ditch
on West Ridge Road,
and then
we heaved them

far as we could into the dump
hoping each would shatter
and that none of our friends
or relatives
would see our stealthy sport.

It was hard work for us,
but a job I enjoyed more than I could tell,

     "a letting go,"

        "a cleaning up."

Each trip, Kyle took his new pellet gun
and B-B gun,
and he shot rats,
and let us—
it's even hard to imagine—
shoot at old bottles
with his precious Red Ryder
(although he wouldn't let us touch his pellet gun!).

I found out
that Karl's a better shot than me,
my vision still a problem,
and my eyeglasses impossible.

Help! ...August

We—Mitch, Brad, Karl and I—
went swimming at the double bridge
down near Pac's today.

The water was clear and cool,
the day hot.
And I remembered Lois King.

It must have been in '44,
when Karl and I were nine.

It had rained hard the night before
and the water was high,
twelve feet deep and swift.

Lois King, a teenager,
and her brothers and sisters
were there swimming, too.

The slippery underwater ledge
west of the double bridge
was our "diving board."

I climbed on the ledge,
dived,
and before I could start swimming
found myself battered
and pulled
underneath the rushing current
gasping for air.

Without hesitation,
Lois King jumped in
and pulled me out,
I not the worse for wear and tear.

I don't think I would have drowned.
I was a good swimmer.

But still....
Who knows?

She, Lois King,
made no big fuss about it.
And we swam
and frolicked
in the cool water
the rest of the afternoon.
The water was so high,
occasionally,
we'd see an old cow turd
float by

uprooted by the water
which broke the banks
and cleaned the pastures.

We called them "cowflops."

Mom and Grandma worried,
as all sane people do,
about polio
(a crippled cousin had it!)
and say the brook's not clean enough,
but we swim there nonetheless.
Active boys think there's nothing sadder
than neglecting a good steam or lake
regardless of the risk.

Lip on Fire   ...August

About eleven,
I was at the kitchen sink
opening a small bottle of Grandma's
homemade root beer.

Stains on the ceiling
reminded me that the bottled root beer,
just like the whale
that swallowed Jonah,
might "blow" again.

I lifted the bottle to my lips,
took a sip,
and cried, "Ohoooooo!"

A big black ant
hiding in shadows on the dark green bottle
had stung my lip.

The pain was gigantic for such a minute villain,

and I danced and jumped,
my lip swelling,
doubling in size.

Hateful ant.
Ballooned lip.

Grandma, Kyle, and Karl
looked at me as if I were crazy!

Lake Compounce   ...August

Yesterday, to mark the end of summer vacation
and in anticipation of the new school year
when Karl, Mitch, and I will be
high school freshman
at Blue Hills High
(Go, Redcoats!),
Mom used a vacation day
and took us to Lake Compounce,
the amusement park in Southington.
(It was like Babb's Amusement Park at Lake Congomond,
but better.)

The day was special, too,
because Grandma Swanson
went with us,
and not only do we want her
to enjoy a day once in a while,
but she buys us extra treats.

We swam in the lake,
rode the little train around the lake
and raced across it

in the powerful,
wave-crashing speed boat.

We did the bumper cars
and spook house twice,
and even rode the merry-go-round,
where Mom says,
when she was young,
she would try to catch
gold rings
for extra rides.

I found,
for the first time,
that I really liked the roller coaster,
it falling away from me
until I thought I'd die.

Mitch had his own money
and rode it two extra times.

My favorite ride of all—
I rode three times—
was riding in the rocket,
the airplane
that hangs out over the lake
on cables,
going faster and faster
until I thought the cables will fail
and I would have to pilot my trusty ship
to a three point landing
far out in the lake.

We rode in the bumper cars,
roller-skated,
and played Skee-Ball, too,
and then went on to the Penny Arcade
where we spent our last coins
shooting corks at ducks
and 22 rifles
at swiftly flying birds of prey.

(Kyle won some post cards
with pretty girls on them.)

We tried to "derrick" bracelets,
combs, rubber jackknives,
and plastic oddities
out of the glass cage
but never won.

I engraved a silver coin:
"Kurt Swanson Thomas, August, 1948."

The day wouldn't have been complete
without those super long hotdogs
with sweet, green relish
and yellow mustard on them.

And then,
one last time,
as the sun began to set,
Grandma handed us more money
and let us ride the roller coaster
and Mom rode, too,
smiling for the first time
since Dad died,

and our solemn Mom,
our dignified Mom,
the CPA,
let out a "Whoop!"

Freshman   ...September

High school is different.
The teachers expect more,
and going from class to class
makes the day more interesting
but confusing, too.

I'm taking English, algebra, physics,
civics, typing, and PE,
a full schedule.

Civics is my favorite class,
Mr. Goodroe, the teacher,
my best teacher.

I enjoy English
but am not familiar
with a lot of writers
others have heard about,
and all the grammar and comma splices
and dangling particles
make me feel

as if I'm the one who needs
splicing to stop the dangling.

There's a lot of poetry
I don't understand,
and Mr. Bill Shakespeare
can be tough going,
old Bill's English
not the one I know.

My hardest class is
physics
with words like:
ohms, watts, voltage, resistance,
and neutrons, protons, molecules, and electrons.

In typing
my fingers have minds of their own,
my words per minute great
until I deduct the billion errors.

Mrs. Langly tells me to be patient with myself,
but there is no patience in me.

Karl and I went to our first dance,
a square dance.

We spent much of the evening
in our flannel shirts and blue jeans
shooting the bull with the other guys.

I did manage to square dance

but *square* is the right word.
I was a "square dancer,"
when I should have "dipsied,"
I "doed."

Still, I think my partner,
Ann Marie, liked me, and said,
"Let's call each other.
What's your numb*er?"*

"3788-J," I answered,
"What's yours?

"2763-M," she said.
"Call me tomorrow
between seven and eight."

Life isn't too bad.
I'm a reporter, too,
The freshman correspondent
for the Redcoat *Courier.*
If I ever learn to type,
I think I'll like it.

I'm a pre-college major.
Karl a *SHOP* student.

He's making a small end table now,
and in a few weeks,
he'll start auto mechanics.

God forbid
that he should fiddle
with Mom's '41 Chevy!

We see Kyle every now and then
when we change classes,
but we don't say anything
unless he speaks first.

School's OK.

"2763-M."
I think I'll call Ann Marie.

Go Redcoats!   ...September

Little Kurt Thomas,
all 130 pounds,
is on the football team.

I'm a Redcoat.

I'm not first-string.
I'm not second-string,
but I'm on the team.

I'll dress for games.
I'll go on football trips
on the school bus.

I may play,
I may not,
but I'll practice
and I'll scrimmage.

Coach says,
"Give it all you got, Kurt.
You're no Kyle yet.
Your time will come."

And so what I lack
in skill and understanding,
I compensate for
with hustle and pizzazz.

In one scrimmage,
I tackled Kyle
and kept him from scoring a touchdown.

Instead of getting mad,
he said,
"You done good, Kurt,"
high praise,
indeed.

I wonder if Dad—
wherever he is—
knows I made the team,
that I tackled his favorite son.

I wonder if he cares.

Karl George and Kurt Swanson Thomas   ...September

Karl and I were baptized
and joined the church today.

Officially, I guess,
we are now Congregationalist
although we've been going
to Sunday School,
and church,
since Cradle Roll.

We were sprinkled.
We wore our new suits,
the ones Aunt Marion
got us for Dad's funeral.

Six of us guys joined the church,
including Brad,
after several sessions with Dr. White,
our minister,
who taught us
"What Congregationalists Believe."

I'm afraid
I don't believe
all that Dr. White believes,
but I guess
I believe enough.

"Kurt SWANSON Thomas,"
I like the sound of it.

Another Accident   ...September

We were hitting a tennis ball
with an old branch,
on our front lawn Sunday,
Mitch at bat,
and the branch broke,
flew toward me,
the pitcher,
and slammed into my mouth
breaking off
a top front tooth.

I spit out blood
and tooth.

Yesterday Mom took me
to Dr. Soderberg's
but nothing can be done.
I'm to watch for abscesses,
and after the swelling goes,
Dr. Soderberg will cap
my broken tooth
with a silver jacket.

Mom said sadly,
"Those things happen."

My tongue is raw
from rubbing
the jagged tooth.

Mom says,
"If it hurts, don't do it,"
but that's easy for her to say.

Mitch felt bad,
but it wasn't his fault,
it was my time,
and my turn.

Raisin Cain   ...October

Last night during our scout meeting.
Brad's father,
our Scoutmaster,
had us hike to Winchell's Bakery,
the bakery that makes
the best jelly donut in town,
for exercise,
and to see how a bakery is run.

David Roberts, our assistant,
went with us,
and we walked fifty paces,
and ran fifty paces to the bakery
half a mile away.

"One, two, three," we counted,
"Forty-eight, forty-nine, fifty,"
as we walked
and then began again,
"one, two, three,"
as we ran.

At the Bakery Shop,
Bobby Winchell,
the older brother,
a "gassed" WW I casualty,
greeted us
with his slurred speech,
"H a a l l o o w, b o y s,"
and Richard, his brother,
enthusiastically showed us
their big refrigerators,
mixing bowls,
and display cases.

Then Richard led us into the kitchen
proudly showing us the six big ovens.

"We get up at three-thirty,"
he explained, and then
excused himself
to answer the ringing phone
in his office, saying,
"Look around, boys,
help yourselves to some of those
raisins on that table."

Hungry boys,
we grabbed some raisins,
and then,
David Roberts,
our leader,
our Assistant Boy Scout Master,
teasingly tossed a raisin
at Freddie Blanchard
and in a twinkling
a raisin fight began.

Several of us were mortified,
but I'm glad to say,
Mitch, Brad, Karl, and I
had no part in it,
ashamed of our pals'
non-Scout-like-behavior.

By the time Richard Winchell
returned from the phone,
there were raisins
scattered all over the floor.

"Boys, enough!" Richard shouted,
and the fight stopped
as quickly as it began,
and we all tried to make amends
by picking up the dirty raisins
and tossing them in the garbage can.

Still the deed was done,
Troop 5 forever tarnished.

Later, in our Scout meeting,
Brad's father got wind of our dirty deed,
and this time,
he with us,
we marched back
to Winchell's Bakery,
apologized,
and sheepishly headed home.

I Don't Know Why   ...October

I don't know what made me do it.
Cobb Garcia came by last week
and joined Mitch, Brad, Karl, and me
in Hide and Seek
in Grandpa's three-tiered barn.

The barn is the perfect place for games.

On one side, there was an empty loft
and under that loft
a wagon filled with sneeze-producing hay,
a favorite hiding place.

In the other half of the barn,
black as ink,
was a another loft filled with hay,
and under that,
milk bottles stacked in crates
safely stored for the local dairy,
a man-made maze of dark, hidden passages.

In one corner
stood an old, forgotten sleigh
and in another, an outhouse
well-used before the house had plumbing.

Above were rafters twenty and thirty feet high
on which we "daredevils" climbed.

Underneath the barn
were cow stalls, horse stalls,
pens that once held pigs, calves, and sheep,
and abandoned farm equipment,
an old corn sheller,
and mowers, harrows, plows, and discs.

Grandpa's barn was the perfect playground
for imaginative, active boys.

We—Cobb, Mitch, Brad, Karl and I—
as I have said,
were playing Hide and Seek and

       whooping,

         hollering,

            running,

               climbing,

                  and jumping

into the hay.

What fun!
Cobb "found" and chased me, yelling,
"I've got you!"
And as I ran from the barn,
Cobb in hot pursuit,
and for some reason,
I don't know why,
I spun around
to slow him, maybe,
and my foot fiercely
caught poor Cobb
in the tenderest of places.

I don't know why!

Poor Cobb, gasped,
then howled,
and fell groaning
and writhing on the ground.

I thought I had killed him.

I don't know why I did it.

Later, thirty minutes or more,
Cobb breathing hard,
in great pain,
and clutching his swollen black and blue treasures,
limped home to tell his mother.

All evening and night,

I waited for her call.
"Kurt, why did you kick my son, THERE?"
"What made you do it?"
"Kurt, I need to tell your mother what you did!"

The hours passed.
My fears mounted.
My imagination worked overtime.

But no call came,
and I wondered
if Cobb even told his mother.

Again and again,
I apologized to Cobb.
"I'm so sorry...,
so, so sorry!"

And still I could not say why,
tell why I kicked poor Cobb,
because I just didn't know why
I let loose with such
a hateful kick.

Football   ...October

The team has played six games
and has had seven weeks of practice.

Practices and scrimmages are tough.
I'm a guard,
a defensive guard.
I've played in two "real games,"
and made two tackles
and missed
six, seven, eight, or more.

But that was OK.
Coach was pleased.
We Redcoats are 4-2.

I wish I knew more about
what I'm supposed to do
and where I'm expected to be
when I'm on the playing field.

Mostly I run and "hit"
anyone who's not a Redcoat.

And I'm as sore as a cob,
as if I've been drilled by angry corn borers.

It's OK.
I'm a Redcoat.

"GO, REDCOATS!"

And Ann Marie has been to all the home games.

Dummy   ...October

For the first time,
Karl, Mitch, and I
didn't dress up for Halloween,
but we did play a
Halloween prank
which almost backfired.

We found a pair of Grandpa's
old bib overalls,
a red flannel shirt,
a pair of mucking boots,
and stuffed them with straw.

We lay the dummy
aside High Hill Road
to see what the motorists
would do
as we hid behind some bushes.

Some ignored our dummy,
some stopped,

looked and laughed,
but our cousin, Barbara, saw the dummy,
and thought it was Grandpa Swanson
deader than a doornail.

When we popped out
from behind the bushes,
she would have killed us
had she been able to catch us
and went to Mom
to tattle about our caper.

Mom,
for Barbara's sake,
scolded us,
no rancor in her voice.

Turn About's Fair Play   ...November

Karl, Brad, Mitch, and I
were playing in the barn today.

While running and jumping,
I got ready to jump
from the loft into the hay,
slipped,
and fell twelve feet to the floor below.

Luckily,
the wooden floor was forgiving,
and I just had
the wind knocked out of me,
but oh what pain!

As soon as Brad
saw that I would live,
he started laughing
and could not stop.

It made me so angry,
I could have butchered him
like one of Grandpa's pigs
until I remembered
how I had laughed at him,
when his bike,
his WW II bike,
his *prefabricated* bike,
collapsed around him,
his legs still pedaling,
and I had laughed.

I remembered, too,
that awful kick
I had delivered to poor Cobb Garcia's
pride and joy.

"Turn about's fair play,"
I thought, as I lay moaning,
mindful of Brad's humiliation
and Cobb's suffering.

Basketball   ...November

I made the Blue Hills squad,
a guard on the freshman team
and dress up for the varsity
although I don't think I'll play this year.

Our freshman team is 2-2.
Coach likes my hustle.

I discovered I'm a better defensive player
than an offensive one,
but drilled some baskets,
one a beauty from twenty feet.

Coach says I'm a "streak shooter,"
sometimes I can't miss,
sometimes I don't come close.

I'm working on that.

I play best in scrimmages,
better nerves I think
when the playing doesn't count.

Still, I'm pleased,
and I love the practices,
playing hard,
making shots
and feeling like
I'm contributing to the team.

I'll never be a triple-threat,
a wonder boy,
a legend,
like Dad,
but I get to play,
and wouldn't want to be like Dad
for all the spice in China.

Wild Animal Refuge   ...November

We Scouts went to the swamp
at the end of High Hill Road
with Brad's father,
the man whose fly rod I broke,
to build a wild animal refuge today.

Wearing hip boots,
we—often falling into the algae-filled water—
jumped and hopped from tuft to tuft,
to the large island
in the middle of the swamp.

We worried about quicksand,
(we knew it was there!)
and thought, if we fall,
we'd spread our arms,
not struggle,
and wait for someone to pull us out.

The refuge was
our Thanksgiving-Christmas gift

to the wild animals and birds.

We built a pole house on stilts
after gathering sticks, grass, and fallen leaves,
and congratulated ourselves
for our "magnificent structure."

We hung suet from it,
and scattered seeds under it,
and hoped
   deer, raccoons,
      rabbits, squirrels,
         skunks, possum,
            red-winged blackbirds,
               ducks, and geese
would have a feast on us,
which we would gladly furnish
once a week.

We will look for signs
and footprints
that tell us
our holiday gifts
have been appreciated.

Poor Mitch   ...November

Last Friday
Mitch went to the hospital
to be circumcised.

He came home Monday.

Karl and I
went to see him today.

Mostly,
Mitch
had the sorest little wee wee in town
and
      paced,
           whined,
                whimpered,
                     and wept.

Nervous Aunt Edith wouldn't
let us get within ten feet of him
afraid we would start roughhousing.

Bossie and the Black Snake   ...November

Last night
I was thinking about
when Grandpa didn't have diabetes,
and he had that cow named Bossie.

Often it was our job
to lead Bossie to the pasture
behind Mitch's house.

Sometimes Karl and I would take her,
sometimes, Kyle,
and sometimes I'd have to go
alone.

Bossie's name was earned honestly,
and although she didn't always
demand her way,
she knew,
with Karl and me,
she could
if she were so inclined.

I didn't like taking Bossie to the pasture by myself.
With two of us,
one could lead her,
and another could
distract her.

I regret now,
that I never milked Bossie.
Grandpa offered,
but that swishing tail
and stocky legs
with flashing hoofs
were all the persuasion
I needed
to let Grandpa do the deed.

But that is neither here nor there.

I started to tell
how, one bright spring morning,
I was leading Bossie through
the pasture
to the place Grandpa
had directed,
when
a giant black snake crossed our trail.
I don't know how long it was,
but it was longer than I was tall.

It seemed to take forever
to cross
in front of us,
Bossie unperturbed,
the black snake

no stranger.

Back home,
I told Karl and Kyle about that snake.
They weren't quite sure,
but were pretty certain
I made the tale up,
or, at the least,
exaggerated.

I wish I could have convinced them
that I told the truth.

Still, today,
I can see that slithering,
sleek serpent
cutting us off like a lazy passenger train
at a gated crossroad.

Second Amputation   ...November

Grandpa's leg
stinks up the house.

They've scheduled his second amputation
for next week.

He doesn't look well.

He's lost his color
and weight, too.

He often has a fever,
is in a lot of pain,
and when he doesn't get his pain killer,
he's crosser
than a bear sitting on a rattlesnake.

Dr. Payne has said
Grandpa's options aren't good

but that there really aren't
any options at all.

He, Grandpa, will just rot away.

So they'll "take" his other leg.

God, it's hard on Mom and Grandma.

It's hard on Kyle, Karl, and me, too.
But, oh, oh so hard on Grandpa
although he tries to keep
a stiff upper lip.

Thanksgiving   ...November

Grandma baked a turkey
but the mood's subdued,
Grandpa so ill.

It's getting cold,
an early winter storm
forecast for this late November weekend.

I'm ready for the snow and ice,
skating, skiing, and tobogganing.

It's too much to ask,
but I'd be more than happy
to lug the double-ripper out
for a spin.

The Ditch   ...December

We went skating at "The Ditch" today,
the Ditch a long, sliver of water
in Johnson's woods behind
West Lane Cemetery.

Years ago, Mr. Johnson, a nurseryman,
had the ditch steam-shoveled
so he could bag the peat
to sell to country gentlemen.

The Ditch is another perfect place to skate,
wide enough for hockey,
and long enough for half-mile races.

Brad, Karl, Mitch, and I
skated there for hours.

We saw a muskrat
and overhead,
a V-shaped gaggle of geese.

After we finished skating,
we ran to the small dump
at the edge of West Ridge Lane
where we had thrown Dad's empty Four Roses bottles,
and looked for treasures,
hunted rats,
and threw rocks
at old tin cans and dirty bottles
for target practice.

Ice Fishing ...December

Uncle Ed took us ice fishing
on Hartland Lake Saturday.

The air was crisp,
the ice hard as frozen steel.

We helped him chip the ice
and ax the holes,
and then Uncle Ed
arranged his fishing types,
their little red flags
ready to spring to life
spread halfway across the lake.

"There goes one!" Uncle Ed would shout
and laugh,
and Mitch, Karl, and I,
our skates flying,
would race to see
who could get there first
and pull in the somersaulting prize—

if still there.

We caught seven yellow perch
and four pickerel,
two good-sized,
and missed several more,
those caught, frozen solid
once they encountered
the frigid, breath-taking air,
Mike Segusa
skating figure eights
around his record player
listening to a waltz.

A+   ...December

We got our grades today,
the last day of school
before Christmas vacation.
My grades were good,
even better than expected.

And in civics, I earned an A+,
the first A+ I ever received,
and "the first," Mr. Goodroe said,
"I ever gave out."

I wonder if Dad ever got an A+ in anything...
drinking... maybe!

Grandpa Dies. It was Time   ...December 24, 1948

We had that Christmas feast
a year ago.

Today even more food
is being carried in
by friends and relatives,
but there'll be no feast.

Grandpa Swanson finally died,
the second operation
questionable, at best.

It had been downhill ever since.

He wasn't the same Grandpa
after the second operation.

After the first,
he complained of *ghost* pains,

shadow pains shooting up and down
his missing leg,
but he had hope
and fought to stay alive.

After the second,
he never felt well,
complaining,
in discomfort,
always in pain,
a tough old man
whose heart
was stronger than his body.
There was no fight in him.

We are all relieved that
he finally gave in and let go.

It was time…
time for him to rest.

Grandpa was not a church man,
and, as far as I know,
not a religious man
either.

Grandpa was a GOOD man.
He worked hard all his life
at the factory
and on the farm.

He help raise seven honorable children,
eight,

if I count the infant who died.

Some say "good isn't good enough,"
but I'll bet on Grandpa.

He'll go where
the good people go
or it's not worth going there.

The funeral will be next Tuesday.

There'll be sadness,
but joy, too.

Everybody is grateful that his pain is over,
the horse-sized shots,
unfortunately,
destined for some other condemned,
unsuspecting soul.

It's Christmas Eve.

There'll be no feast,
but Bless Us in our Sadness
Bless Us All in our Great Sadness,
and Bless Grandpa
most of All.

Christmas Day   …December, 1948

We opened presents today.

Karl and I were given those B-B guns
and barely cared.

We would have put off
the gift giving,
and the gift opening
if Grandma had not said,
"That's not fair.
Let's do it for the boys."

We were sad,
sad as I can ever remember.

Friends and family came by.
They hugged, and kissed, and said,
"I'm so, so sorry," and cried.

Some even said,
"You boys will have to be
the men of the family now."

Grandpa's body
is at Benson's Funeral Home.

But Grandpa is not there!

I know he's looking down on us,
on Grandma,
on Mom,
on his other sons and daughters,
and on his twenty-one loving grandchildren
and knows
that he is worthy
of our love.

Loose Strings   ...Christmas, 1949

A year has gone by
since Grandpa died.
It's Christmas Day.

We are back into a routine.
Grandma keeps busy,
sewing, cleaning,
and cooking.

The house smells of corve,
lutfish, fruitsupa, head cheese,
sill and potatoes, anchovies, and sardines.

Aunt Marion still comes every Monday
with sightings of new wildflowers,
helps with the washing,
and she and Grandma swap tales.

Our dog, Romeo
is KING now,

Grandma's Mitsi
crippled with arthritis.

I can see that look in Romeo's eyes.
He'll soon start his travels
to do what he does best.

Aunt Edith, Uncle Ed, and Mitch
came over for Grandma's Christmas feast
last night,
Uncle Ed on crutches
after he fell from their roof
replacing shingles,
his left leg broken
and in a cast.

Aunt Edith hasn't seen another
copperhead,
but she is just as nervous as ever.

Mitch is taking accordion lessons
and has a talent for it.

Mitch got a sleek,
motorized
cart for Christmas.

Mom's doing OK,
working, working, working.
She wanted Dewey to win,
but I liked Truman.

I keep wondering if Mom will start dating,
but I don't think that will happen.

She must think,
"Why take the risk?"

Uncle Fritz brought his fiancée,
Bertha Cunningham,
by last spring,
to meet Grandma.
(Uncle Fritz was wearing a shirt!)

She's nice,
but a talker,
so she and Uncle Fritz
should do fine
because he's
a talker, too.

They are going to get married
in March,
a private ceremony.

Grandpa Thomas
is doing fine.
He's playing pool,
and hanging around with his old cronies.

We see him now and then
but not as often,
and we seldom see Uncle Kurt.

Cobb Garcia and his family,
including his gypsy mother,
are moving to New Britain.

I hope they sell their place
to someone who will let me
skate at the Marsh
as often as I like.

Karl's into electricity now,
in Shop.
I hope he doesn't burn the house down.

He hasn't tinkered with Mom's car,
at least not yet.

He and Beth Judy,
a pretty cheerleader,
are going steady.

Karl was the second baseman
on the Redcoat baseball team
and batted .335.

Go, Redcoats!

Kyle got his driver's license
on his birthday
and is a popular part-time worker
at New Britain General.

Like Dad,
in one Redcoat game,
Kyle scored two touchdowns.

My big news
is that the town's Boy Scout troops
had a speech contest in May
and Kyle and I represented Troop 5.

Kyle came in second
and was Fireman of the Day.

Old Kurt,
Yours truly,
the god damn SOB
who could not do anything right,
won First Place.
I was Mayor of the Day
and a photo
of my ugly mug
was in the newspaper
and a big story about me, too.

ME! MAYOR OF THE DAY!

Then, for deviltry, I wrote a story
poking fun at myself as Mayor
inaugurating silly town laws
which were featured
in the Redcoat *Courier*:
"No jaywalking on Chamberlain Highway after midnight."
"Pet owners must clean up all their dogs' messes
if their dogs do their *business*

on their neighbors' lawns."
"No couple shall hold hands until they are eighteen."
"No legally blind driver shall drive a school bus."
"School principals may paddle students
only if they themselves have been paddled for
their mistakes."

My feature was so well received
that this SOB
is now a regular columnist
for the Redcoat *Courier*.

During the summer,
Karl, Mitch, Brad and I
held a circus on Uncle Fritz's hilltop lawn,
and Mom's boss,
a circus enthusiast,
showed slides of famous clowns—
like Emmett Kelly—
on a sheet hanging
between two poles.

Karl and I acted out a skit,
Karl, wore a set of rabbit ears
Aunt Marion made for him,
and I wore an old bear costume
from some past school play.

We were a big hit
doing our
"Rabbit with the Bear Behind" routine.

From April to September
I mowed cemetery plots
at West Lane Cemetery

and earned $7 a week.

(Mr. Josephowitcz must have found
another hiding place for his whiskey
because I have not seen him there.)

In July, Mom took
a day off from work
to see her brother,
our Uncle Walt
in Milford.

He owns a small yacht
and took us sailing,
Grandma, too,
on Long Island Sound.

Karl, Kyle, and I appreciated the little cruise,
but we loved

      swimming around the boat,

           jumping,

                    and diving into the water
from the deck of the yacht
when it was anchored
about fifty feet off shore.

We were intoxicated by the smell
and taste of the salty sea.

On the way home,
Mom bought us
goat's milk ice cream
which she loved as a child.

Kyle ate some,
just to please Mom,
but Karl and I
barely tasted ours
and thought it was nasty.

In October,
Karl and I went hiking behind West Ridge Lane
and we saw
a big white-tailed deer
running through the sand pit,
and I wondered
why anybody would want to shoot
anything so magnificent and majestic.

That reminds me,
Kyle still won't let us shoot
his precious pellet gun.

Karl's B-B gun is broken,
and I've lent mine to Brad,
our appetite for B-B guns
receding.

I was second-string tackle
on the football team
and learned a lot.

Our record was 6-3.
Coach says that with the first-string tackle
graduating this year,
I should be a starting tackle next fall.

"Go, Redcoats!"

I wish I could brag about my basketball play.
As a sophomore our new coach seldom played me.
He had his favorites,
and I wasn't one of them.

I hope things go better next fall.

Dr. Pemberton is still working on my teeth.
I had my first root canal in May
and a second in November.

Now I'm gun-shy going to the dentist,
so much pain and aggravation.

The tooth that broke off
has a silver cap,
and some of the guys call me
"Wolfgang."

This coming summer
I'm going to be an apprentice counselor
at the Boy Scout Camp
near Westwood.

One of my jobs
will be to teach young Scouts
how to paddle
and maneuver canoes across the lake…
after I learn myself.

I wonder what Dad would think of that,
his god damn Kurt, a canoe instructor.

My grades continue to be
better than acceptable,
but I got a B- in geometry,
confused by obtuse hypotenues.

I've learned that life goes on,

                           has its

                                        ups and downs

now and then.

My nightmares
aren't quite so severe,
the rocks and boulders
still rush toward me,
but not so often.

At least I've not seen
another angel…
unless it's Ann Marie.

"2763-M, Please!"

Printed in the United States
1269400004BA/200